Fox Woman Dreaming

By
Joy Voigt

ISBN: 9798498233093

Written by Daniela Joy Voigt

Edited by Johnathan Back

Cover art by Mareano Ruíz

Cover design by Albert Strasser

Inquiries can be directed to joyisintheheart@gmail.com

Please visit www.mandalasproject.com for further information

Reviews help authors immensely. If you enjoy this book,
please consider leaving a review on Amazon.
Thank you.

Also by Joy Voigt

On Becoming Human (Poetry)

Alchemy of Love: Savory cookbook
Heart of Joy: Sweets cookbook

For Anthony,

the murderer, the willing sacrifice,

the edge of the woods, the love in the raw darkness,

and never a prince charming.

Listen to the story told by the reed,

of being separated.

"Since I was cut from the reed bed,

I have made this crying sound.

Anyone apart from someone he loves

understands what I say.

Anyone pulled from a source

longs to go back.

At any gathering I am there,

mingling in the laughing and grieving,

a friend to each, but few

will hear the secrets hidden

within the notes. No ears for that."

From "The Reed Flute Song"
by Jalāl al-Dīn Rūmī,
translated by Coleman Barks

Chapter I

o o o

"Listen, Sybil. Listen to the sound of my voice. Anchor there. Listen."

There is ash on my hands. I can feel the delicate substance dance through my fingers in its unusual weightlessness and almost liquid form. A smell is here of rotting vegetables and a warm hearth. I feel the earthen floor beneath me and am comforted immediately by the feeling of home.

"Sybil, listen, listen carefully. Describe what you see around you."

"I see wooden walls surrounding me. I am inside a room. There is a gentle breeze flowing through this building. I feel comfortable here. I sense that I have lived and worked here my whole life."

"Very good, Sybil. Well done. Now it's time for you to play your Bridgepiece for me, honey. Play it now."

My eyes have become more accustomed to the dim light now. I can feel the cold, steely, familiar feeling of the Bridgepiece in my warm hands. I hesitate for a moment. Something in me wants to pull away from his voice. Something in me wants to do the opposite of what he is asking me to do. I struggle. Inside me there is a cascade of wriggling confusion.

"Sybil....Sybil. Stay with me, darling. Listen to my voice, anchor there. All you have to do is play the Bridgepiece for us. You be a Good Girl now and do as I say."

Warm again. Good Girl. Yes, that is exactly what I am, a Good Girl. I can do what he asks of me. I would do anything he tells me to do. He loves me. He has my best interest in mind.

I take the metal piece, with its familiar handle and two prongs. I feel its weighty density in my hands and hit it against the wooden table next to me.

"Well done, darling. Well done. I am so proud of you. You are such a Good Girl."

I am filled with a familiar sensation. A resonating vibration fills my body from head to toe and I find myself smiling, for no reason, into space. My mind is blank. I am completely malleable.

"Darling, concentrate now: tell me your name."

The smile vanishes. I am no longer tingling. My mouth is grey. There is a terrible, loud clanging in my ears. I have the sensation of worms crawling on the edges of my teeth. My tongue has become vast and thick, like an obese eel trying to escape the caverns of my mouth. I am dizzy and can just make out his voice. But I know what he is asking me. He has asked me so many times before. I know what he wants to hear, I know what he wants me to say. The eel is making moves, it is trying to highjack my throat, and I have to wrestle it to make it say what I want.

"My…My…My n…na…name is. My name is Yeh-hsien."

"Yeh-hsien. Good. Very good. OK, dear, it is time to go outside now. Tell me what you see."

I gather my skirt around me and make my way to the wooden door. I go over the threshold and am instantly marinated in the golden warmth of the afternoon sun. I have the taste of honey in my mouth and my legs seem to float over the well-beaten earth around me.

I look up and see my father. He is coming toward me, smiling, I believe. When I try to focus on him, his face morphs from shape to shape, one moment having a broad countenance and bushy eyebrows, the next a slim face with a wide grin.

"Yeh-hsien, that is your father. You know that. Relax your concentration now, do not focus on the face. Remember you are never meant to focus on anything. Just let it be there and move on. Who else is there?"

Resistance again. I find in me the wish to stare at this man's face, to lock eyes with him and let his features wash over me in familiarity. But something else in me knows that this is Bad. And I don't want to be Bad. So I reluctantly look away and find another face.

I gaze past my father and see her. She seems to be surrounded by a sea of steam. I try to find her face. Again, a mutative collage of facial features dances before me, all of them laughing and sneering. I avert my gaze quickly and find myself speaking through muffled lips, "Stepmother." Beside her, suffused in the same coiling steam, stands another feminine figure. Stepsister.

"Okay now, look down at your hands, Yeh-shien, what do you see?"

"A golden fish."

My hands feel slippery. I look down, a golden goby is swimming between my fingers and I find myself delighting in its graceful movements. Everything around me stops. Fish scales catch the light of the sun and shimmy in a hypnotic dance that leaves me enthralled. The piscine form seems to melt into my own skin and it is hard for me to distinguish where I start and where the goby ends.

"Very good Yeh-hsien. Tell me, who gave you this golden fish?"

"My mother did, before she died."

"Yes, yes she did. And now what is happening?"

"Stepmother is coming closer to me. She takes the golden goby from me and hands it to Stepsister who, in an instant, dismembers the fish before my eyes and tosses me the lightweight bones. I am crying."

"And what do you hear now, Yeh-shien? What is that sound you hear?"

"I hear a female voice coming from somewhere in the distance. The voice is golden, like the fish. It wraps itself around my body and speaks, 'Take these bones, my child. Take them with you. Whatever you want you will have, you only have to ask.'"

"Good Yeh-hsien. Tell me now, whose voice is that? To whom does the golden voice belong?"

"My mother."

"Yes, your mother. Like all Good Girls, your mother will always be there to take care of you. Isn't that right, sweetie?"

I find myself nodding as if in a trance. Yes, Good Girls are always taken care of. I'm a Good Girl, I will always be taken care of.

"You are doing very well, darling. Now, look around you Yeh-hsien. Where are you?"

"I am back in the earthen room with wooden walls. Time has passed, but it is hard to tell how much. I feel like I have been here forever. My body is hungry and I remember the fish bones. I am on the floor and remember what my mother said. I am asking them for food.

When I turn around, I find a small feast under an earthen pot. I am thirsty. I ask, my thirst is quenched. I am cold. I ask, I have a hearth.

"Outside there is the sound of trumpets and music. I can hear the large bustle of a crowd gathering. The local festival is here. I try to look out the window but Stepmother is standing there."

"What does she say to you, Yeh-hsien? Tell me what she says."

"She tells me that I do not belong at the festival, that I am too awful and ugly to go, that my presence there will dampen the greatness of her beautiful daughter and herself. She gives me a list of tasks to do

and expects them all to be done by the time she gets back. She tells me that she will beat me if I do not do as I am told.

"I watch Stepmother and Stepsister, along with Father, leave, dressed in silks and their finest jewelry. I am left behind, alone.

"I hear the fish bones rattle in the corner. I take them in my hands and find myself speaking to them.

"I am standing now, a gust of wind has pulled my dirty dress away. I gaze down and am enrobed in a beautiful gown that sings through its stitches. Every pearl embroidered on the fine silk glistens with ecstatic beauty. The dress knows itself to be exquisite and holds my body in regal charm. I look around me and my chores have all been done. The door has creaked open and I find myself stepping outside."

"Where are you now, Yeh-shien?"

"I am at the festival. Beautiful men and women laugh and smile. Everything smells of lavender and hydrangeas. Every texture I behold seems to be made of velvet and ebony. Every object I behold radiates merriment. The very floor beneath me pulsates with pleasure. My body is light and the air wraps me in its enchanting weightlessness, as if inviting me to sway in its embrace. I am, for the first time in a very long time, happy.

"I see her. Stepsister spies me in the crowd. Her eyes are boiling, her body is spiteful, she is a venomous creature about to pounce on her prey.

"I turn and flee, running as fast as I can. My body is heavier than it has ever been. I seem to be sinking into the earth beneath me. I can barely breathe and, when I try to turn my head to see the one who chases me, my neck stays locked in place, as if frozen in terror.

"I lose something. I can sense it, but I do not know what it is.

"I have run for a long time and am now home. I lock myself in my earthen room and clutch my fish bones close to my heart."

"Good, good Yeh-hsien. What is happening now?"

"I hear the distant sound of a clarion. It keeps getting louder. It is coming closer and closer."

"Yes, yes, Yeh-hsien. The clarion, very good. Tell me what it says. What is the message it brings."

"It is the clarion of a great noble man. He has been searching far and wide for someone. He has something that belongs to that someone, he found this object at the festival. He has searched and searched and failed for so long. He is tired but determined. He must meet whoever owns this object that he carries with him."

"Very good, very good. Now tell me, what is the object he has?"

Again, a glimmer of resistance. My mouth wants to run away. But I am Good. I am Good.

"He has a shoe. A very small shoe, for a very delicate foot. He says that the woman who has such small feet must be the fairest woman of them all. He says that he is searching for this fair maiden to make her...to make her..."

A pang, a pang so deep the soles of my feet curdle.

"What, Yeh-hsien? What does this noble man want?"

The taste of iron fills my mouth. My fingernails dig into my palms. I feel the tiny pores on the back of my neck bristle like a wild wolf.

I am Good. I am Good.

"He wants to make the woman with the small, delicate feet... his wife."

"Good girl. Good. Now tell me, Yeh-hsien, tell me what you see when you look down."

I don't want to look. I know what I will find, I know what is there. I knew it from the moment I opened my eyes in this place, the tell-tale signs that I have been avoiding all along.

"Yeh-hsien....Tell me now. It's okay."

My eyes are going blank. Breath is becoming agitated.

"Yeh-hsien, come on now, dear, sweet one. Tell me what you see."

There is dirt on my tongue. The wind around me gets cold, the walls seem to coagulate and shrink.

I force my neck to bend and I look. I look at what I already know.

"I...I...see that my feet....my feet are very delicate and small."

"Brilliant! Absolutely brilliant! I am so proud of you! Tell me, darling, what is happening now?"

"A crowd has gathered outside Stepmother and Father's house. I can see the nobleman from where I am standing by my window.

"Stepdaughter is dancing in delight. She is showing off her delicate feet to Stepmother. She is buoyant and giggling in that strange way of hers.

"The group of people have gathered closer to the house, they murmur with excitement. The nobleman stands before her and is holding a small shoe. Stepsister sits down and, elegantly, lifts up the

hem of her skirt. Her smile is as big as the sky. She is staring at the nobleman with wide eyes and shows him her small foot. He smiles for a moment and then kneels down.

"She seems to be delirious. Shoe is being slipped on, sliding on, almost fitting but then, the heel refuses to give. Stepsister pushes, budges, makes herself bleed. She muffles a cry, the air around her quivers. The nobleman gets up and walks away without a second glance, he seems to be broken.

"In his despondency, he is walking straight towards the earthen hut. He is coming towards me. My hair is standing on end. I know what is going to happen."

"Where is he now, Yeh-hsien? Where is the man?"

"He is right in front of my door."

The air is filled with the smell of chrysanthemums. The floor beneath me feels like a bed of golden fish scales. Something inside me is shimmering. I feel electric, scintillating. My body seems to be gyrating in small elliptical movements and my cheeks are flushed. My palms are hot, my tongue feels alive and hungry. He is at the door. I can feel his hand on the doorknob, the weight of his bones and the texture of his hands almost touching my own skin and bones.

"Good, Yeh-hsien. Tell me what you see now."

"He is opening the door. I am about to meet him."

The door is creaking. A floodgate of light blinds me for a moment but I can see the silhouette clearly: a body cloaked in a large golden robe, as if made of fish scales; the brow is high and noble; the eyes are deep set and oceanic. In a flash I know, this is not the Prince searching for his bride. I look down, trying to make out the rest of the body…and as I gaze down on the chest, I pause for there is a very clear sign of…of breasts.

¨Sybil! Sybil! You devil of a woman. Bad girl, bad. So Bad. You get the hell back here now, you hear me. Play your Bridgepiece right this moment. Wake up! Get back here now!¨

I find my hands moving unconsciously as I play the Bridgepiece. My body's weight is fading. My eyes are slowly closing. I can feel everything shaking, gyrating in a chaotic dance. The figure is still at the doorstep, grinning, almost foolishly, waving at me as I am slowly ripped away.

¨Open your goddamned eyes! That's enough of this circus now. I am not going to be degraded by your nonsense anymore! Wake the hell up.¨

Wilhelm's hands were wrapped around Sybil's shoulders and he stood there, violently shaking her and swearing. Beads of sweat were cavorting on his wide forehead, some of them trying to hold on to his moistened skin for dear life and others, the reckless kamikazes of the bunch, were heard yelling "Geronimo!" as they threw themselves into certain death against floor, wall and unto Sybil's still unconscious body. Even for the untrained eye, it was obvious that this man was profoundly stressed.

She came back to with a shudder. It always takes a while for a Dreammaker to remember who and where they are and, usually, enough time is allotted for their mind to reorganize itself so as to ensure they stay in functioning order. It is too much of a burden to deal with a Dreammaker who loses their marbles due to Identity Regrouping Failure.

This time, however, Wilhelm did not have the patience to give such treatment to this particular Dreammaker and he berated her as her eyes droopily tried to make out the contours of the all-too-familiar Office.

"You little devil! How many times have I told you what your duties are? All you need to do is follow my voice, anchor to the Bridgepiece and then follow the script. How hard can it be, Sybil. Seriously? I have had enough of your charades and Management is breathing down my back with serious concerns about our performance. Our ratings plummeted since last week's show and the Consumers are starting to complain. It's not difficult, Sybil, it really isn't.

I've worked with so many Dreammakers before and no one has ever been such a pain in the ass to deal with as you. Did you skip your medication today? Is that what this is about?"

Wilhelm grabbed Sybil's bag and rummaged through the insides. He pulled out an orange bottle filled with pills and muffled a curse word.

"Your goddamned medications, Sybil! Why the hell aren't you taking them? The one thing The Company asks of you, the one single thing that you are responsible for, and you can't do it." Wilhelm let out an exasperated grunt and then added, "You are given everything, Sybil, everything."

Wilhelm's eyes slowly became bloodshot as he continued, "Remember who you were before this? Remember? You were starving, freezing and thirsty. You were so close to dying that The Recruiters had to pump you up with liquid food and medications just so you'd make it through the night. And now look at you! You want anything to eat, anything at all, and you have it at your beck and call. Fine wines, fancy drinks, anything you can imagine, you have it. Remember what you were wearing for that whole winter before you came to us? A plastic bag, Sybil! A disgusting plastic bag! I mean it, look at you: manicures, pedicures, false lashes. Look at what you are wearing now! There is not a single woman that would not die to have the things that you own. And how do you show your gratitude? By being a negligent, ungrateful miscreant, that's how. The Company gives you everything you could ever want, and this is how you repay us. I can't believe you. This is the last time I'm enduring this, Sybil. Next time you give even the slightest inkling of going off script, I am reporting you directly to the Director and then you'll really face the consequences of your actions. Now get out of my sight, I can't bear to even look at you anymore."

Sybil's mind was still Regrouping, but she tried her best to get out of the reclined chair she had been lying in. She disconnected herself from the Media Outlet, grabbed her things, and dragged her heavy feet out the door.

Chapter II

o o o

Waiting for her, standing outside in the corridor, were Anne and Bella. Anne had with her the all too familiar handbag that held within it an endless cornucopia of sweets, ointments and floral teas.

"For whenever you need a little pick-me-up," she would always say, chirping contentedly.

Sybil looked pale. Being connected to the Media Outlet was exhausting and, everyone knew, you needed at least three days to recuperate from the experience. Being Woken Up was not a common protocol and its effects ravaged the nervous system of any Dreammaker.

Anne and Bella were quick to hold Sybil up and then looked at one another nervously.

"What happened, dear? Are you okay? Was Mr. Grim a little too demanding on you today? He's got a lot on his mind these days, you know. Please don't get angry with him." It was Anne's distinctly sweet, motherly voice who spoke.

Anne's voice had been whipped out of merengue and corn syrup and left to marinate in liquid taffy. It had such caloric weightiness to it that Sybil had once jokingly told Anne that, if she kept talking to her in that tone, she was sure to give Sybil diabetes. Anne had smiled. After all, she had been trained to become that sweet. It was nice to receive that reassurance.

At the moment though, no matter how many molasses-laden sentences Anne could muster, Sybil was completely dysfunctional and incapable of articulating a response. Her limbs swam around her, her eyes distorted all shapes into brown, formless blobs. She was quickly losing her footing and balance.

In an instant, she fainted.

Back in her room, Sybil lay in bed, oblivious to everything around her.

Anne bustled about, rearranging random objects, humming thoughtless melodies and looking over at Sybil's unconscious body in fretful glances, only to then move nervously on.

Apart from the honey-strewn speech that Anne had perfected, she had also mastered the art of smelling like freshly made home-baked goods no matter what time of day it was. Her dresses were stitched with lace and her face, round and pudgy, had its own gravitational pull. For five consecutive years now, at the Ceremony, Anne had been given the award, "Model of Motherly Perfection."

Bella was in the room too. She sat at the edge of the bed and silently watched her friend breathe in and out, matching her own inhales and exhales to make sure that Sybil did not miss a beat.

It was not until late into the night that Sybil opened her eyes again.

"Oh my, child! You had us all worried sick about you. Now come here, have a taste of this soup, it will bring you back to us in no time and will clear your mind of any unpleasant or unwelcome thoughts," said Anne as she came closer to Sybil's side.

Anne held a bowl of herb-smelling soup ready for Sybil, and she slowly spoon-fed her back into consciousness.

The voice is always the last thing to come back after being hooked up to the Media Outlet. Somewhere in the back of Sybil's throat, her words lay wilted and dazed, looking at each other in bewilderment and heavy from the day's events. After some time though, Sybil managed to mutter something intelligible to her friends.

"What, dear, what was that?" Anne got closer and Bella strained to listen.

"I....I saw....him." Sybil's words sputtered and landed in the middle of the room, where Anne and Bella quickly caught them and put them away, under the rug.

"Now, now, sweetie." Anne was patting Sybil's head, smiling reassuringly and continued, "You must be having a little bit of trouble Regrouping, that's all. It happens to the best of us. It's okay. Nothing to worry about. We're here. We'll take care of you and then we can put all of this in the past. You'll be back in working order in no time. We'll practice and memorize your script, we'll work on your ratings, Mr. Grim will adore you, the Director will sing your praises again, and you'll be everyone's darling once more. Everything will be back to the way it used to be and we'll all be happy again. You'll see."

It was strange for Sybil to hear Anne's words. She knew that she meant every last part of it. She knew that Anne would care for her, she knew that Anne wanted her to be happy, what's even more, she knew that Anne loved her. Anne had become like a mother to her over the time she had spent at the Company, always ready to hug her, feed her and hold her. But the words sounded hollow. Oddly too, she felt like she had heard these words before, as if this whole scenario she was in had happened already and she was simply repeating a well-rehearsed role.

It was Bella who pulled her out of her musings.

"Anne is right, Sybil. This is just a little hurdle to get over, no big deal. Everyone has their adjustment period, for some it comes earlier and for some it comes later. You haven't been in the Company for that many years, it was to be expected that you'd run into a little trouble. You were on a winning streak for so long: receiving so many awards, prized by the Director, loved by the Consumers. You were bound to come across a little difficulty eventually. But not to worry, we are here for you. We are all here for you. Every single Dreammaker is cheering you on. We all want you to win and come ahead, Sybil. Truly, you were created for greatness."

Sybil tried to remember her training. Comfort. Comforting words, they were there to help any Dreammaker face turbulence. They were there as a safety net for when confusion might enter the system. They were there to make everything Good and Nice again. And everyone likes it when things are Good and Nice. Yes, Comfort.

Sybil sat up straight for a moment and looked at her friends. Then, in a voice that was oddly too cheery and upbeat for her dizzy state, said, "The two of you are right."

She nodded vehemently and held herself up by grabbing onto the side of the bed with both her hands. She then added, "Thank you. Thank you for being so kind to me and for your endless generosity. Even when I am not doing the Right thing. I don't want to make anyone mad. I want to make everyone around me proud, especially the Director. No one has ever shown me as much kindness as he has. I would have died had it not been for him. I promise to mend my ways. I'm sorry."

Anne and Bella beamed at each other and then looked lovingly at Sybil.

Anne hugged Sybil and said, "Everything is going to be all right, dear. You'll see."

Chapter III

o o o

The stamp on the time-card read "5:30".

"More Contribution Time this week, X0720?" It was Consumer S233 who was asking, standing in the queue, holding his briefcase in one hand and smiling.

"Indeed, S233. My boss appreciates my work so much that this is the fifth time this week he has asked me to donate some of my time to finish this project. We have big deadlines, you know, and I love being able to serve. I feel so lucky." Consumer X0720 put away his time-card and turned to his colleague.

"I wish I were as lucky as you, X0720. My boss has only asked me to make three Contributions this week. I'm going to try and do better, work harder, be less distracted. I want to become an Outstanding Citizen like you some day."

"I applaud your virtue, S233. It's intentions like those that keep our Society running. I am sure you will be able to Contribute more soon. Just keep at it and persevere. You'll see. That's how I did it. I started off at the bottom of the ladder, working five days a week and, I am almost embarrassed to say it out loud now, but getting a full paycheck for all my work hours." X0720 shuddered for a moment at the memory, "But then I continued to prove myself over and over again to my boss, showing at any chance I got how much I wanted to serve our mission, how much I was willing to give everything for my job. And then recognition started coming my way. Soon, my paycheck got smaller and smaller. I was asked to stay one day a week for Contribution Time and now, look at me, I get to serve our Society every day of the week because of my perseverance. You can do it too, S233. Keep your hopes alive. You'll see it will all come to you one day."

S233 smiled and took X0720's words to heart. He had two full Tuning Days to strengthen his determination and, as soon as the Work Week started again, he was going to do everything he could to prove himself to his boss.

"Thank you for the inspiration, X0720, truly."

"My pleasure. Now, enjoy your Tuning Days, I'll see you next Work Week."

X0720 turned and made his way into the bustling street. The familiar sound of other Consumers making their way back home, getting ready for their own Tuning Days made X0720 happy. He loved knowing that everyone was doing their best and that all of his hard work paid off and was creating an efficient, hardworking Society that he was proud to belong to.

He stopped off at the Refreshment Center to buy some of his favorite meals: two Afternoon Boosts and two Evening Delights. He paid for his purchases, put the small packets in his coat pocket and made his way down the familiar streets that took him back home.

His apartment was long enough for him to take eight steps in any direction, the regulated size for any human habitat. The kitchen consisted of the Zapper and the Cooler. There was a small bathroom at the far end of the square space with his bed right next to it. And, in the middle of the room, a large Stream Screen sat gloriously, like a kingly toad, dusted and pulsating, imbued with a vitality of its own.

In front of the Screen there was a small sofa, indented with X0720's body shape, that stood shyly in the room, bashful at its aesthetic condition.

X0720 made his way toward the Cooler and placed three of the four packets he had just purchased in it. The fourth one, one of the Evening Delights, he set on a tray which he then placed inside the Zapper. He always loved to press his face against the Zapper's clear screen and watch the packet go round and round, parading itself before his entranced eyes and then slowly transforming, expanding as if by magic, into his favorite food. X0720 sometimes felt embarrassed, being able to witness such a metamorphosis right before his eyes. He felt like an unwelcome voyeur. It seemed like he should not be allowed to watch such majesty unfold.

When the timer went off, X0720 pulled out the tray and the smell of yellow cheese, pasta and butter waltzed luxuriously out, lavishly pressing itself into the corners and walls of the room, leaving a trail of plump dairy odor in its wake. X0720's mouth responded in turn, a little pool of saliva forming on the top of his tongue and, taking a fork, he took his tray and prepared to settle into his well-worn seat.

The sofa creaked under X0720's body weight. It tried to mould itself to his contours, but so many years had gone by now in this way that it barely had any moulding capacity left. For tonight, it contented itself to simply prop X0720's body up. In the end, it was all it was capable of doing anymore.

X0720 tucked mightily into his dinner, letting out small grunts of satisfaction and dribbling small trickles of yellow substance down his chin. Had someone been looking carelessly on, one could have imagined that X0720's chin had been vandalized by graffiti-painting hooligans, such was the artistic mark that the phosphorescent cheese substance was leaving on his skin.

The Remote was in the exact same spot where it always was, conveniently placed on the sofa's armrests and easily accessible at any moment. He always timed his return for his favorite Stream on the Bella Channel.

He pressed the On button and let out a tiny burp which got whisked away and then stuck on the old wallpaper draping the room. He then put his empty tray down on the floor and settled deeper into the recesses of the sofa's worn out springs. For the trained listener, it was easy to hear that the sofa sighed and muttered some intelligibly depressed remark, such was its lot in life.

The Stream Screen's vivacious colors and entrancing lights stood at odds with the rest of the apartment. Prancing pinks and obscene yellows, vivacious greens mixed with aquamarine blues emerged from the Screen and bullied the browns and grays of the walls and furniture into submission. The apartment and its contents cowered in the corner as the Screen's portentous paraphernalia took over the small space. X0720 may have squealed in delight, but would be too embarrassed for anyone to know.

Bella's face appeared on the Screen, with her deep blue eyes, her high cheekbones, her delicate neck and that impossibly blonde hair that tantalized and beckoned anyone that came into its visual reach.

X0720 had watched the News recently and seen that Bella had been awarded, for the seventh year in a row, the prize of "The Beauty." It was no surprise to him as he sat there, eyes unblinking and dribbled cheese congealing, that this was, without a doubt, the most beautiful woman he had ever seen.

The familiar soundtrack started to play and Bella's face began to crack open into a wide, warm smile. X0720's neck cradled itself into the sofa's headrest and the subtle sound of the Tuning started to pour from the Screen's speakers.

A memory appeared to him, just a moment's flash. He had the image of his parents coming home from a Work Week, sitting down to eat their Evening Delight and…could it be? Yes, yes it was. The look of his mother, smiling and laughing as X0720 tried to crawl onto her lap. And then, that sound, the same sound that he was hearing now, and how his mother's smile vanished in an instant, wiped off, eyes blank, head back, cold to the touch. He remembered her looking straight ahead at the Screen, his father too and X0720's small voice saying, "Mamma."

He knew he had made a mistake because, as soon as the words came tumbling into the living room, a hard hand smacked him across the face and his father's furiously furrowed brow along with his single index finger in front of his lips roared at him, "Shhhhhhhh!"

Could that be? No, he must be mistaken. Maybe the food packet had been expired. Must be. But, somewhere inside his ribcage, X0720 felt a pang of something he was unable to describe. Perhaps the pasta was causing him instant indigestion. Yes, perhaps. But no, he knew indigestion all too well. This was different, it was as if his lungs were trying to collapse on him for a moment. He could feel a sigh wanting to be birthed within him, but too many years of Tuning warned him that one should never allow such a thing.

His chest was shaking mildly and, from his eyes, a gentle mist was threatening to break free. No! This simply could not be. He knew better than this. He was an Outstanding Citizen, for Goodness' sake. He had heard of some goons, miscreants and fools, people who lived far away on the outskirts of the Capital who talked about these kinds of experiences. Saying such lies about Consumers. Even blaspheming and saying that Consumers could have emotions! The nerve. And not to mention the absolute nonsense that one of them had said that time so long ago, something about not trusting the Tuning. X0720 chuckled. What a ludicrous idea. He wondered how he had even started thinking about such absurdity.

No one ever took any of these people seriously. None of them had even appeared on any of the Channels. None of them were even mentioned on the Stream Screen. Obviously they were flawed creatures that did not belong within Society, so why would anything they said ever even matter. He even doubted if any of these people existed. People living outside of the Capital? What insanity, what depravity. Impossible!

Obviously this was the pasta talking, doing some misdeed inside his system. Obviously. Everyone knew that Consumers did not have emotions, did not have thoughts of their own. So this could all be explained as some mechanical defect that he could just ignore and move on from.

Head back in place, arms on the armrests, feet square, he stared ahead and let himself be washed over by the sound of the Tuning. This time, no misfit memories tried to wreak havoc on his mind. The dulling sensation and muting of all sounds other than those coming from the Screen started to take over him. A half smile poked its head through his face and a tiny rivulet of drool rappelled down the side of his lip and onto the floor. And, on the screen, Bella started to speak.

Chapter IV

o o o

Once upon a time, in a land far, far away, there lived a wise king and beautiful queen. They were wonderfully kind and generous people, fair to look at and warm of heart. They were Correct and Moral and held the Law to the highest of standards, making their land the purest and most law-abiding in all of the four directions."

Bella's voice was like a pot of warm cardamom jam on a cold winter's night. Her consonants cradled themselves into her listener's ears and her vowels wooed her audience into a thoughtless stupor. Riding on the waves of her mezzo voice, she continued to spin her tale.

"The king and queen were incredibly happy and all was well in their kingdom. Even the trees and the animals were eternally content on their lands. There was harmony and bounty for all those who dwelled under their reign.

"Only one thing placed a shadow in their seemingly eternal spring. Only one thing remained dark. A secret they held between them in hushed tones and soft susurrations: they could not bear a child.

"And so it came to pass that many years went by and the people of the kingdom started to murmur amongst themselves. Rumors began to sprout from the marketplace and its vendors. Hushed whispers scurried along the back alleys, and worry started to take root in the hearts of many.

"The king and queen, seeing that there was unease and unrest, sent a messenger to recruit the wisest people of all the land to aid them in their plight. On the seventh day, thirteen crones arrived to the court.

"It so happened that the first crone to arrive was indeed a wise and kind fairy who, upon seeing the king and queen and their great misfortune, granted the queen the gift of fertility. With a touch of her hand, the queen's womb began to grow and, within the hour, a small child, a little girl, was seen running and laughing in the once silent castle walls. Such was the delight of her merry presence that the stones themselves were heard giggling and her small running footsteps echoed through happy hallways and overjoyed towers.

"The king and queen were so jubilant and gladdened that they immediately arranged a large feast to be served, full of wild and exotic dishes, such was their wish to repay the fairy's kindness. The tables were set and, on them, cascades of creamed morel pudding poured forth, stuffed artichoke leaves glistened, and flasks of elderberry syrup as well as endless fountains of fermented poppy liquor gushed onto the floor. The scents of the banquet polkaed their way through the hallways, randomly adding a two-step for flare. They foxtrotted their way down the drawbridge and finally twirled off into the town and beyond.

"Being kind and generous as they were, they invited all the crones to the feast. However, even in the opulence of their court, the king and queen had a limited number of places at their table and could only fit fifteen guests. The king and queen took their seats and had their newly welcomed daughter take another. Then twelve seats remained and each crone, according to the order in which she had arrived, took her place at the feast.

"And so, in this way, it was that the Dark Crone, the crone who came from the farthest reaches of the kingdom, in that place where the Sun refuses to play, was left standing. Now, one must know about this crone that she had her pride and she had traveled long and far to answer her king and queen's request. She was tired and hungry and not very happy with the situation at hand. It would also be useful to know that, just as the first crone had been a fairy, this crone was, in fact, a witch.

"Witches will mind their own business as long as one does not bother them. Had she been left alone, this witch would have been off in her stone hut concocting her wild spells: turning bears into princes or giving young maidens mustaches. But it would not have gotten any further than that small mischief. Now, however, the witch had had to put her own life on hold, travel on horseback and endure the endless yapping of the messenger who had come to fetch her, had now been offended in front of others, and was having a hard time keeping her cool due to her hunger. So, trouble was brewing.

"It was the young new princess who drew the witch's attention. The young girl was playing with her guava pudding, squeezing it through her tiny hands, and was completely unaware of what was happening around her.

"The witch got closer to her and asked, 'Little one, pray tell me, what is your name?'

"The young princess looked up with empty eyes and locked her gaze into the witch's unblinking stare.

"It was the queen who answered, 'Good grief woman, can't you see, this child is just a toddler. She does not know her name yet. I shall tell you. Her name is Aurora, Aurora the Fair.´

¨The witch smiled in the best possible way that a witch can smile, crookedly and strangely unappealing. As much as she had tried to practice her smile in front of the mirror, this was always the result. 'Well, Aurora,' she said and then looked up to address the whole court, 'Your parents have made a grave mistake today, darling. They have shown complete disrespect to me and my powers and, for that, they will have to pay. I hereby cast a spell on you, condemning you to a luxurious and blessed life until the day you are to turn sixteen, whereby you will come across a spinning wheel and on it, a spindle. You will be so enchanted by it but, upon touching it, you will surely die.' And with that, the witch walked out the castle doors and made her way back to her stony hut, leaving an unhappy court behind her.

¨It was the fairy who spoke up and, trying to lighten the mood, said ´And so it is that blessings turn into curses but, in the same way, a curse can turn into a blessing. I cannot destroy the witch's spell but I can give it some modifications. I hereby change the spell so that, upon the princess' sixteenth birthday, she will touch the spindle but, instead of dying, she will be put into a great and powerful sleep that can only be broken by the kiss of the man who truly loves her.

¨Although the king and queen were still despondent, the feast went on. Princess Aurora continued to play with her food and the whole kingdom was once again happy, for the time being, to have a princess among them.¨

Chapter V

o o o

I am holding a long string of unspun cotton in my hands. I can feel the delicate fibers tickling my skin. The room is dimly lit, the air is heavy around me."

"Good, good. Now, Aurora, tell me what else you see in this room."

"There is something in the corner. I can hear the sound of wood pressing against wood. As I come closer I can see a spinning wheel swiveling out of control."

"What else do you see, darling?"

"Something is glowing, an incandescent, small spike. I can barely make it out, it is shining so brightly. But I can see it now, I know what it is: it is a spindle. I can't take my eyes off it. I feel magnetized to its shape, it draws me near. I feel locked into its gravity, my whole body is called towards its sharp, pointed form."

"Now Aurora, tell me what happens. Tell me what happens when you get closer to the spindle."

"I...I...I can't resist. I reach out my hand to touch it then, instantly, I am flooded with a feeling of being put under water. I feel like my head is swimming in a sea of algae, my limbs are endlessly long, my body has become pliable and limber.

"I hear a scream in the distance and my mother, the queen, is by my side, shaking me, crying out my name. I cannot open my mouth, I cannot seem to tell her that I am here, that I have not gone anywhere.

"The guards are at the threshold, they are picking me up. They are taking me to a tower and I am now resting in a large, soft bed. Everything around me is quiet. The dust itself is starting to settle on already settled dust. The objects in the room are becoming old, convalescent, many of them filing for pensions and planning their retirement. I can hear my mother and father come to my door and hide their sobs over and over. The room itself is drowned in sorrow, the sobs hanging in the air, making the room pregnant with heavy tears, until it is claustrophobically sad. The room is oppressive and, finally, both my mother and father stop coming to my side. I am alone.

"No one is near me, no one is coming to see me. Even the insects in the room have lost interest. The walls around me are bored. I am alone, completely and utterly alone."

"Yes, Aurora, you are very much alone. No one is caring for you anymore. This all happened because you touched the spindle, remember that. Tell me now, what is happening in that room? What do you hear now?"

"My ears have become unaccustomed to sound, everything has been buried under a pile of feathers. But I can make something out now, a voice is floating outside my door. The voice is becoming louder, more distinct."

"A voice, indeed. Tell me, who is this, who is the owner of this voice?"

"It is Him! It is Him, I know it is. I have been waiting my entire life for Him to come. I have waited patiently for Him. I have laid in this bed and done nothing but wait for Him. It is Him, it is Him!"

"Who, Aurora, who?"

"Prince Charming."

"Wonderful, Aurora. Absolutely wonderful, describe him to me."

"He is perfect. Absolutely perfect, tall and strong and so handsome. He has come into the room and I can feel the strength emanating from his body. His eyes are so kind and his hair is so perfect. He has perfect teeth and perfectly strong hands. I want him to come near me and he does.

"He is leaning over me now and speaking to me gently. I cannot make out many of the words he is saying but I can feel the tenderness in his speech. I feel what he is saying through my pores, through the tips of my fingers. I can sense what he has come here for."

"What, Aurora, what is he there for?"

"He is here because he loves me. He is here to set me free.

"I feel his strong body lean against mine and my mouth has become an aquarium of sea creatures. My lips are oat stalks in a wild field caressed by a warm summer breeze. My skin is dancing the cha-cha and between my legs …"

"Ehem…yes, yes. So now. He kissed you. Very good. What happens next, Aurora?"

"Oh…um….my eyes! My eyelids are fluttering open. I can see again! I look into his deep blue eyes and I know I love him too. He is my Hero. I am coming back to life. The room around me is awake again, outside I hear the sound of birds singing and inside me there is endless warmth. I am awake and all I want is to be his wife."

"Absolutely wonderful, Aurora. Now, we are coming close to the end here, what happens now, dear?"

"We are dressed in fine clothes and I am walking down an aisle. Everything around me smells of dahlias and roses. The room is decked in white and my prince is smiling at me before an altar. We hold hands and make eternal vows to each other. I promise to be a loving, loyal, kind and unconditional wife. He promises to take care of me and protect me. We kiss and we are married, bound to one another until death do us part.

"We are now king and queen of the land and our subjects are all smiling happily at us. Every creature on our land is merry again, everything around us seems to glisten."

"Good, good. Now, what is the last thing we need to say now, sweetheart?"

"And then, then we lived happily ever after...The End"

"Bravo, bravo! OK, now, relax, my dear. Breathe now. And, tell me, what is your name?"

"Aurora."

"Good. Now, play the Bridgepiece again for me, won't you? Play it for me, sweetie, play it."

"I am playing it."

"Good Girl. Darling, tell me, what is your name?"

"Bella."

"Bella, good. Listen, Bella. Listen to the sound of my voice. Anchor there. Listen. It is time to come back now. Wake up, Bella. Wake up."

Jacob's voice lassoed Bella's mind back from where it had gone. Like a veteran cowboy, his voice pulled her back, tethering her as she made her way through the maze-like corridors of her awareness and back into the Office.

It was always the first few seconds back that were the hardest. She lay there, blinking her eyelids open and shut, as if trying to persuade shapes to squeeze into her eye sockets. But she knew better than that by now. It was just a matter of time, nothing she could do could ever make the return easier.

She felt an imperative pounding on her temples and nausea was knocking at her door, trying to get front row seats to her stomach.

Jacob sat by her side, impatiently. He was never thrilled by how long it would take a Dreammaker to get her bearings back. He'd been in the business too long to be gentle and caring anymore. The younger the Dreammaker, the more impatient he would become. And, although Bella was a beauty to look at, Jacob had too much to do that day and too much on his mind to accompany her while she came out of her stupor.

"Ok Bella, we're done for the day. Think you can get up now?"

Knowing full well that she couldn't, Bella still attempted to get to her feet. Jacob disconnected her from the Media Outlet and ushered her out the door.

"See you next week, Mr. Grim," her words wiggled lazily out through her parched lips and fell, in a semi-comatose state, on the threshold of the doorway.

"Yes Bella, see you next week." Jacob was ready to go back into the Office but then remembered something he wanted to mention and turned back, "Bella, just one more thing. Your witch for this Stream was, well, how shall I say it, she was a bit mediocre. She was a bit soft, not obvious enough in her Motif. Remember Bella, Consumers depend on us. Streams are the only way that Consumers will not fall into utter depravity. It is our duty to teach them what is Right and what is Wrong. If we do not give them clear Morality, if we cause confusion in them, it is our fault. You would not want to confuse our precious Consumers and plunge them into utter despair now, would you?"

Bella shook her head vehemently and said, in almost a whimper, "No, no, Mr. Grim, I would never want that."

"Good Girl, that's what I want to hear. I am making some adjustments to the script. The witch will be more clearly Evil for our next Stream and I'll be taking out most of your ad lib. Work on memorizing this new version for me, won't you?"

Bella nodded and then felt quite weak. She could have used a reassuring arm at this point but Jacob had turned around and closed the Office door behind him. She drowsily made her way back to her chambers.

Once Jacob was back at his desk, he pressed the intercom button.

"Wilhelm?" The voice on the intercom came through in short bursts of static.

"Jacob, yes. I'm here, buzz me in."

Jacob and Wilhelm were the highest grossing Tellers in all of the Company. They had spent years studying the Consumer's behavioral patterns, analyzing Consumer's schedules, making graphs about Consumer's preferences and had, for a long time now, been avidly following the Company's highest rated Channels to find what it was that the Consumer most wanted to see. As brothers, they had come to understand many of the ins and outs of the Company and Walt, the Director, had been very pleased.

However, as Wilhelm stepped into the Office, Jacob could tell that he was deeply troubled.

"What happened last week?" Jacob asked.

"That rascal Sybil again. I'm telling you, Jacob, there is something seriously wrong with that girl. I thought she would be the best of the best. I groomed her. I groomed her like none other. I monitored what she ate, how much she exercised, what she wore, how long her nails were, who her friends were, everything. Everything! It was working so well for so long. Remember how she won her first award in her first year here?"

Jacob nodded.

"First year award! Who has ever heard of that?"

"Well, there was that one time, but it's hard to know if any of that was true because Mag…"

Wilhelm shot Jacob a dirty look, so dirty indeed that Jacob was cut short and left his sentence hanging midair.

Wilhelm swept aside the sentence, watched it scamper off into a corner and continued on as beads of sweat once again started to mingle and exchange niceties on his forehead, "Look Jacob, I am reaching my last straw here. Last week's show was so ludicrous, so outrageous, that our ratings went down by another five points. Everything was going fine and then, out of nowhere, Sybil just goes off script and has this absolute nonsensical ad lib where, you know what she said?"

Jacob shrugged.

"Instead of Prince Charming coming to the rescue, like she knows he's supposed to, like we've done a hundred times before…" Wilhelm's voice gets tight and constricted for a moment, he swallows hard and then continues, "Some bizarre character comes along. And, I can't even say this with a straight face. You know what she describes?"

Again, another shrug.

Wilhelm looked at Jacob straight in the eyes and said in exasperated tones, "She said he had breasts! Breasts, Jacob. What in the hell? Are you kidding me? Where is she getting this crap from? At this rate, we're going to be history in no time. And the Director, the Director sent me a warning last time and now, I haven't even heard from him. I bet he's fuming. Damn it, Jacob! We were doing so well, what went wrong?"

Jacob stood up and said, "Honestly brother, I can't really say. You did a textbook grooming with her. She should be, by all means, our highest rating show. She was doing so well at the beginning that I started to believe she might be the best show the Company has ever had."

Wilhelm's shoulders dropped furiously and one tiny sweat bead threw itself, like a liquid lemming, off into the precipice.

"I don't know where she got this idea from, Jacob, but I found her pill bottle almost half full. I suspect she hasn't taken any of the medication we have given her in the last month. How could she even think of doing such a thing?"

Jacob was stunned. He had never heard of something like this happening before. Bewildered, he looked out the Office's window.

"Listen, Wilhelm, this is a case like none other. We need to be extra vigilant, we are too high profile around here. If we fail, we will be sacked in no time. Let's get her back on her medication and give her a little vacation time. Pamper her, make her feel special again. You know, they all love that stuff, it gets to their heads and nothing is easier to manage than puffed-up pride. You'll see, brother, we'll figure this out."

Although feeling internally bleak, Jacob's words served to relax Wilhelm a bit. He had trusted his brother in many past endeavors and, though many of their ideas had seemed wild and unpredictable at the time, they had always succeeded. Perhaps Jacob was right, perhaps not everything was lost. He patted his brother's back and managed to nod the smallest of nods.

Chapter VI

o o o

P at-a-cake, pat-a-cake baker's man, bake me a cake as fast as you can. Mix it and stir it and bake it just right, good from the first 'til the very last bite. Write his name with lots of care and make pretty flowers here and there. Pat-a-cake, pat-a-cake baker's man...¨

It was Anne who was singing under her breath. The song spilled over her flour and eggs, mixing itself into the dough, then making its way into the oven, through the cooking berries and baking itself into the crust of the three pies that Anne was lovingly making for Sybil.

Anne's Stream was coming up in two days and she wanted to make sure that Sybil had enough food to keep her well fed while she was away. Although Sybil was entitled to get anything she wanted from the Company's Nutrition Center, Anne knew that Sybil had a soft spot for her baked goods.

As she wagged and wiggled through her kitchen, she began going over her latest script. Charles, her Teller, had sent it to her and she was enjoying this new chapter of her career. For many years, she too got to have a Stream like Bella's. She was young and charming and a perfect fit for the Princess Motif. How she had loved having a Prince Charming and the gowns and the sceneries. Princess Streams always had the most views, so she had been very popular for a very long time and had much success within The Company.

She remembered when Charles gifted her her favorite blue gown, as well as the shoes and jewelry that went with it. She would get so many gifts from so many adoring Consumers, it was hard sometimes to keep it all in her chambers.

Then she remembered the day that Charles had called her into the Office and when he told her that it was time for her to change her look. He had been so kind, so gentle. Bless him. She would do anything he asked. Of course, of course she would change. And so her skin became a little softer, her wrinkles started to show, and her whole body became a pudgy, gentle, edgeless shape that she would perfume with neroli oil and dress in lace. She was happy to get a new look, she had said to Charles, but the lace had to stay.

For some time now, her scripts had changed and she had had to learn to rhyme and sing. Charles had told her her voice was perfect for this new format. He said their ratings were going up again and that they had a whole new audience tuning in: the very young children of the Consumers. He told her she was perfect for the Mother motif now.

The oven timer rang and Anne wiped her hands off on a perfectly folded towel. She put on her oven mitts and pulled out three perfectly made thimbleberry pies, Sybil's favorite, onto the cooling rack on the table. Pie smells undulated off of them in a starchy dance and seduced Anne's nostrils into a sniff or two.

As Anne let the pies cool down, she found herself searching through the rooms of her mind and found her first memories of Sybil.

She must have been no older than sixteen. How thin she had looked. Her face was hollow and distant, like a feral cat, she thought. She could see Sybil's bones protruding out of her worn out skin and the smell, good grief, the smell. Sybil seemed to reek with the stench of mouse guts and sad urine.

She heard the words the Recruiters called her: "crazy", "hysterical", "mad".

Something in her disliked those words. They did not appear to be suitable words to be saying inside the beautifully furnished hallway of the Company. They knocked into the walls, they left their dirty fingerprints on the fine porcelain vases, they stuck their tongues out at the finely polished people in the room. She shuddered for a moment.

Anne had been in the Company for so long she could hardly remember when the Recruiters had come to find her. It felt so far away now that she wondered if any of that had ever even happened. She tried to recall her life before the Company but it was a white-washed set of lost memories that felt like they belonged to someone else.

When she had stood there, looking at Sybil in her ragged state, she wondered if she had ever looked so base, so uncouth. Her hands went down to her skirt in her familiar tic, and patted down the sides of the material, ironing out the invisible wrinkles.

It was Wilhelm who asked Anne to take special care of Sybil. At first, it seemed a useless task. Sybil appeared to be so…so uncivilized. There was something strange about her. She remembered how it had taken her ages to convince Sybil to wear any clothes. That wild girl would wander around the Company, stark naked, oblivious to her onlookers and obviously unaware that her behavior was having a negative impact on all those around her. And her eyes, those deep wells of mystery, dark and peering, as if they had been made of the very bottom soil of the darkest forest, in that place where mud sings its inhospitable tunes, her eyes inhabited a different ecosystem. She recalled how they would peer out at everything around her, as if she were looking out from some cavernous rut, observing everything, taking it all in and not speaking a word. Anne remembered gazing deeply into Sybil's eyes a day after she had arrived and, try as she might, it was as if they were speaking another language, utterly foreign and exotic to anything she knew.

There was something unique about that Sybil girl, especially during her first months at the Company. Something, something Anne could not quite put her finger on, as if Sybil were a kind of…Nonsense. No, Anne knew that what the Company said about Sybil was true. She had not had the privilege of being Tuned as a child like everyone else had, she was to be pitied, and cared for, she needed to be nurtured back into health, back into sanity, back into Correctness.

Strangely though, Anne had never been quite able to put the thought away that Sybil reminded her, in the oddest of ways, of a wild animal.

Enough time had passed now, however, and Sybil had had enough Tunings, enough trainings, enough time within the good and competent hands of the Company, and things had settled down. Bella, Anne and Wilhelm had been by her side the whole time, bringing her back to health, aiding her in anything she needed.

Anne smiled as she remembered the first time she saw Sybil dressed in a gown. How different she looked, she thought, from that first ragged creature brought in from the streets. There was an elegance to Sybil that Anne had never seen before. Not even Bella had that level of grace. There was something about Sybil that one could never quite define, but it lived in her, it pulsated through her skin, down to the tips of her untamable brown hair, like an electric current that howled within her. Sybil was a voltaic shock bottled up inside a human body.

Anne let her memories fade into the background and went back to her dough. As she folded and tucked and shaped and baked, she began humming, in her matronly voice, her latest script, "Mary, Mary, quite contrary, how does your garden grow? With silver bells and cockleshells and pretty maids all in a row. And pretty maids all in a row..."

Chapter VII

o o o

Sybil had received Mr. Grim's note some days ago and was relieved to find that she would be taking a break from her Stream duty for a week. Although she had been told that Streaming was part of her service to Consumers and it was, truly, the reason for which the Company took so much care of her, some part of her had always felt some resistance to the experience.

But, she thought, she must put all that resistance aside now, do as Anne and Bella had recommended, and let herself be pampered and cared for this entire week. Not a lot of Dreammakers get treated the way she did, they had told her.

She was making her way down the corridor, toward the Beauty Lounge, dressed in her mahogany robe and fuzzy slippers.

Of all the clothes she had ever been given at the Company, these were, by far, her favorites. She loved the feel of the soft material against her skin, and the smell of wild fibers that could not be hidden under any perfume. At times, she had come to even think of her robe and slippers as her wearing a kind of pelt. The idea made her happy.

Such were her thoughts when a Beautician escorted her onto a plastic bed and asked her to take her robe off. Lying there, Sybil remembered the first time she had ever come to the Beauty Lounge and had this same procedure done for the first time.

She recalled the feeling of the hot wax against her legs. She thought she might be having the same experience a candy apple must have when dipped into hot sugar. The kind Beautician with the pretty face had asked Sybil to relax and breathe, that all of this was worth it, that pain was beauty and beauty was pain.

And then, the ripping began. Sybil tried to choke back some tears, tried to control herself, but all she wanted to do was to bash the pretty little Beautician's teeth in.

Anne had told her that, over time, the pain would subside and that she would see how beneficial this all was. Consumer analytics showed that a woman without hair was much preferred over a woman with hair.

Sybil agreed to the whole thing eventually but always wondered about removing the hair between her legs, in that strange place that no one ever talked about. She liked that little untamed tuft of wiry wilderness. In particular, she liked the smell it had, like that of an undomesticated moor or of half-wilted bougainvillea blossoms. She recalled the days, way before she had come to the Company, when these little rebel hairs started to sprout there, how she had played at giving them hairdos and how funny it all was and…

Oh, oh no. She had been told many times that remembering her days before the Company was Bad. She had to stop herself immediately. She let the memory go, let it escape into the Beauty Lounge, let it be waxed off her mind. Forgetting now. And then, for a moment, bewildered, she wondered if that memory was even true.

Sybil was pulled back from her pondering when the Beautician asked her to look up at the Stream Screen. Above the plastic bed was a large sleek, sheeny Screen. From where she lay, Sybil felt like the Screen floated above her, enveloping her in its silky aura.

The now familiar sound hit her in a flash, her head sunk deeper into the bed, her eyes locked forward, and Anne's beaming face appeared, smiling, on the Screen. Anne's Stream Music came on as the credits rolled. The familiar name of "Charles P., Teller" went by as well as the characteristic font reading, "This Stream brought to you by Evening Delights. Remember to eat right and keep a healthy schedule to serve and continue to perform well. You too can become an Outstanding Citizen." Sybil could see how Anne's face in the background continued to smile vehemently through it all.

Once the credits had finished, Anne's voice, mellow like licorice syrup, came through the speakers, and Sybil's eyelids drooped a little as she listened, "What are little girls made of? Sugar and spice and everything nice. That's what little girls are made of..."

The Beautician cleared her throat a little and then whispered to Sybil to take a deep breath. Sybil did as she was told, gulping air into her lungs, gritting her teeth, and trying to fake a smile to make it all easier and then rip, rip, rip.

Sybil got off the plastic bed, feeling more naked than when she had arrived, slipped back into her robe and proceeded to sit down at a table to get her nails done. The other pretty Beautician there talked about the latest analytics and what the biggest Beauty trends would be for the upcoming season. The Beautician's voice bounced and wiggled of its own accord, making its way into Sybil's ear canal and preparing itself to have a pajama party there.

Once her nails were done, the same bouncy Beautician took a look at Sybil's pores under a magnifying glass.

"My, my, Miss Sybil. This is no good at all. What have you been doing to yourself there, honey? Are you getting enough of your Beauty Sleep? You know I told you last time, you need at least eight hours of total Non-mental activity to keep your skin looking young, radiant and healthy. It's what the Consumers want, Miss Sybil. And who are we to go against the Consumers, I ask you? You better get yourself some very good rest, Miss, otherwise we are going to have to go in with skin injections sooner than we thought."

Sybil listened and thought about her nights in the past month. As much as she tried to go into Non-mental Mode, she just could not. Too many images came to her. She felt like she was wrestling her mind every night and, far from being rested, she woke up every morning feeling like she had gone to battle. No wonder her pores were not looking particularly flamboyant and perky.

"I know, I know. You are right, I am trying my best, Alana. I just...I just keep having these images at night. This man keeps trying to tell me something and...."

Alana, the Beautician, squeaked in fright and, in high-pitched tones said, "Sweet Darling Baby of all that is Good and Right save us now! Now listen here Miss Sybil, I don't want to hear any of this business. I'm not that kind of person! I know when a good thing is good, and this here

Company is good to all of us. The Company is good to you, the Company is good to me. And I know for a fact that any thoughts that come at night are pure and utter nonsense, brought to us to keep us from doing what is Right and Moral. I like you Miss Sybil, I really do. I have watched your Stream every week for many years now. My husband, good and righteous man that he is, he thinks you're wonderful too. We have been your fans now for a very long time. We even have one of your posters in our home. I'm not sure about what all has been going on for the last month with you, Miss. Strange things on your Stream coming on, but I think we can all have our bumps on the road. Who hasn't? We all know you were very young when you began, and maybe that has something to do with it. I don't know, I'm not smart enough to figure things like that out. But I do know that you're pretty and famous now. And I know that Beauty is here to make us succeed. You will make it through this, Miss Sybil. I know you will."

Alana smiled widely at Sybil. The magnifying glass was still between them and Sybil could tell that Alana's pores too, were less perky than usual. Oh well, she thought.

"Thank you, Alana. You are so kind to me. You're right. You are completely right. I *am* starting afresh. Look, I'm here now, aren't I? Show me the trendiest toenail color of the season, won't you?"

Alana clapped her hands in glee and seemed to do a little tap dance in place. She reached out to get a bottle of Magnetic Blue out of the nail polish cabinet and said, "I've been dying to give you a pedicure, Miss Sybil! Positively dying!"

Chapter VIII

o o o

My breath is feral. I can hear myself panting. My skin exudes
the scent of musk and undomesticated mud. From afar, I hear the sound
of a loon wailing in its crazed laughter at the Moon. It is dark, but my
eyes can see perfectly. I am running close to the ground. I can feel the tall
grasses hit against my body and my muscles feel tough, crisp,
instinctual.

My ears are perked up, my body is ready to leap, I am taught
as an instrument's string. And then, I see a shimmer in the distance.

I look out from behind a pile of sticks where I have hidden.
The air around me smells of chrysanthemums. He is there, dressed in
golden fish scales, scintillating under the Moon's beams.

I search inside my throat and find a howl wanting to erupt. I
open my mouth wide and...

Sybil's yowl filled the chamber walls and Bella fell off
her cot, waking her up instantaneously, in utter confusion.

Bella had been asked to stay with Sybil through the night and to report anything unusual to her Teller, Mr. Grim. She found that it would be hard for her to explain exactly what had happened that night.

Sybil was sitting up in her bed, sweating ferociously. The yowl had woken her up too and she was completely disoriented. Her hair was standing on end and, from her body, there exuded an acrid smell of fermented camphor and unusual sweat.

Bella was uncertain of what to do. She had never seen Sybil like this before. Actually, she had never seen anyone in a state such as this before. Having grown up with Good Parents and Tuned her whole life, Sybil's behavior fitted none of the compartments of what her mind could come to comprehend.

She stumbled around the chamber, unclear of whether Sybil was even aware of her presence. She watched as Sybil bleated out a couple of yelps and then curled up into a tight ball, shivering and quaking.

As she stood there, baffled, all Bella could think of doing was what she had seen Anne do many times before and she began to hum a little ditty in the softest of tones.

Sybil's ears twitched and her breathing began to soften. Bella took courage and made her tune a little louder, taking a step towards the bed.

¨Twinkle, twinkle, little star. How I wonder what you are…¨

Sybil's body exhaled and Bella continued, ¨Up above the world so high, like a diamond in the sky…¨

Sybil's eyelids opened again, fluttering like drunken butterflies, and Bella sat down by the foot of the bed.

¨Twinkle, twinkle little star…¨

Bella's hands found Sybil's feet. They felt frozen and moist, as if drenched in forest dew. She gently touched them, warming them with her body heat. Her voice continued now, more confidently, stringing itself inside the tight ball of Sybil's frame, ¨How I wonder what you are…¨

Sybil exhaled even deeper and her body began to unwind, uncurling, and finally lying flat on the luxurious bed she had been sleeping in.

Bella got closer and put her hands on her friend's head, combing Sybil's hair with her fingers.

¨Sybil?¨

¨Yes…Bella…¨

¨Sybil, are you…are you okay?¨

Sybil leaned into Bella's hands and let her massage her forehead and temples. She spooned her body around the perfectly contoured edges of Bella's extraordinary figure and seemed to wrestle deeply about what to say.

"Bella. I...I...I'm not sure how to say this but...I've been having images at night."

Bella's hands stopped mid-caress. She felt a cold quiver go down her back as her spine quaked and trembled. Gulping and feeling scared she said, "What...what do you mean, Sybil, images?"

"Yes Bella, just that. I lay down to sleep like I've always done and then, at some point in the night, I stop having Non-mental activity and images come into my mind. It is always the same image: I am in a forest and everything is covered in luminous moss. There is something inexplicably appealing about my surroundings. I am magnetized by the feeling sense I have of everything around me. It's like I want to bathe myself in the vegetation around me, drink in the night air, become inexorably mixed with the earth beneath me. My body is not quite this body I am in, it's different somehow but incredibly familiar. I feel like I am at home and I..."

Bella was trying hard not to push Sybil away. Never in her wildest thoughts could she have imagined things getting this far. As she looked down at Sybil's feverish face, she felt a warm wave of care. She had come to love her friend. And she knew it had not always been that way.

She remembered when Sybil had arrived to the Company and how everyone seemed to be mesmerized by this unclean wild beauty that came up with the most unusual and adventurous Weaves. She remembered how so many of the Tellers begged to be put on her case, to be able to do the Extractions, to ride on Sybil's success.

Until then, Bella's Stream had been the most popular Channel in the whole Company. Everyone knew her name. Tellers would come up to her hoping to get to work with her. Beauticians would queue up to work on her body. Not to mention the amount of gifts the Consumers would send her: champagne dipped chocolate, pumpkin flavored cotton candy and, her favorite, glazed nasturtium petals.

Wilhelm had been her Teller for so long by then that she could not imagine her life without him. But then, when Sybil arrived, Wilhelm dumped her in an instant, leaving her with his much less handsome and much less brilliant brother, Jacob.

She knew Wilhelm was ambitious. She knew how much he wanted to be the best rated Channel, the most well known Teller. But she had come to believe that Wilhelm cared for her, that his words were really meant for her and not just part of a pre-written script that he had to say. She missed him calling her, "sweetie" and "darling."

But he thought he saw something in Sybil that no other Dreammaker had. And when Wilhelm asked Bella to become one of Sybil's friends…her heart almost broke. She felt betrayed, used, treated like a plot device instead of a protagonist.

Wilhelm had been right though. There was something about Sybil, something no one had seen, at least not in her lifetime, that made her skyrocket to the top in no time. Perhaps Wilhelm had been right all along. And since her own Stream's ratings had gone down, she figured she'd take the friend route and be successful by association. At least it was better than being forgotten.

But now, even that was in a frail state. When she looked down at the strange woman she was cradling in her lap, she felt suddenly confused and slightly disgusted. She could not figure out what to say to keep her friendship intact but also to keep her own sanity unscathed. She could not fit what Sybil had just told her into anything that she could manage mentally. Sybil's words felt like unwelcome hooligans trying to wreak havoc to the insides of her well-manicured thoughts. She feared the worst, that what Sybil's was saying might come to unstitch the delicate thread-work that kept her mind in perfectly correct and functioning order.

She swallowed hard and tried to remember her training. Comfort. Just Comfort.

"There, there, Sybil dear. Listen now, my sweet friend. You are like a younger sister to me and it worries me to see you like this, believing such trivialities and nonsense. These things you just said, they must not be true in the least. Who ever heard of images while we are in Non-mental activity? These are all old wives tales, not to be believed in the least. The Company has proven over and over again that such things do not exist. I know you are a smart girl, a Good Girl, I know you can understand and distinguish Truth from Fiction. Think now, Sybil. Is what you just told me true?"

Sybil's head was swimming, doing a frantic doggie paddle to try and stop itself from drowning. Not true? What she had seen was not true? She was making it all up? None of this existed?

Bella was patting Sybil's head now and repeating the words, "It can't be true, dear, none of it could be. You know better."

Bella had been her friend throughout her whole time at the Company. More than a friend, actually. Yes, an older sister, a role model, a perfect example of how to be Good and Moral. She had taken so much time to take care of Sybil when she knew nothing about how the Company worked.

She remembered the first time Bella told her about the Weaves and explained what it was that was happening to her. She remembered Bella holding her hand as she walked her to her first Extraction and how she had been so proud of her. She remembered coming out of that first experience and being so bewildered by the whole thing. And how Bella had patted her on the head, just as she was doing now, and combed her hair with her fingers, just as she was doing now. And how she had laughed merrily as her fingers got stuck in the many knots in her tresses and said, "Sybil, you should have taken Mr. Grim's advice and cut all of this untamable mane of yours off and gone for a wig!"

She could trust Bella. How many times had she heard in her training that one cannot trust oneself, that we need others to point out the way, to guide us into Rightness. That must be what was happening. She was being tested. She was being tested to see if she would actually know Truth from Fiction. Yes! She knew the answer now.

Bolting upright she said, "Bella, you are right. I can never trust the images that my mind creates. They are the breeding ground of all that is Bad and Immoral. I have been being tested to see if I will hold my ground, if I will follow my training. And I am. I am!"

Sybil hugged Bella and she, in turn, sighed in relief.

"Wonderful, Sybil. Mr. Grim told me you might have some trouble come round during your sleep, that is why he sent me to be here with you for some nights. He also told me that you had neglected taking your medication so, Sybil, will you be a Good Girl and take it now? I think it will help you sleep better and go back to the restful Non-mental activity that you so deeply seem to need."

Saying that, Bella pulled out a medication bottle and popped out two small, round pills that she then handed to Sybil.

Without a second thought, Sybil took them and swallowed them. Within a minute, her vision became blurry, her head gave up on trying to stay above water, and she was sound asleep in Bella's arms, who patted her head one last time and tucked her in for the night.

"Don't worry Sybil, soon all of this will have passed."

Chapter IX

o o o

She's ready, Jacob."

Wilhelm stood, erect and immovable, looking out his window at the rows and rows of residential buildings that neighbored the Company's headquarters. His tone was dry, and it made Jacob fidget in his seat a little.

"Bella just informed me that Sybil has taken her medication every day without any coaxing or incentive from either herself or Anne, and she has been keeping all of her Beauty appointments diligently."

"Well that's great news, brother. Are you going to do a Stream with her this week?"

"No, Jacob, I'm not. Bella told me something that I have found quite unnerving. She told me Sybil has been seeing images at night and, although she tried to repeat it to me, to tell me what Sybil had said, it was complete incomprehensible nonsense. All she could make out was something about a woodland, and something about a man. I could not make heads or tails of any of the rest of it."

Jacob fidgeted in his seat again, which caused it to squeak, filling the room with a high pitched sound, like a penguin giggling or a jovial puppy hiccuping. It was greatly distasteful to Wilhelm, who assumed the tone of this exchange to be held in utter silence. This was a serious conversation. He turned his head and gave a menacing look to his younger sibling.

After clearing his throat, Wilhelm continued, "Bella mentioned some very unusual behavior. Sybil woke up in a fit, she could barely speak for some time, but what she did manage to do…" Wilhelm had to clear his throat again, his eyes looked down, words seemed to find hiding places in his throat and tongue. He had to coax out his speech and said finally, almost inaudibly, "She apparently managed to let out a loud howl."

Jacob's marrow stood at a halt, something deep inside his intestinal region tried to scurry and dart into hiding, and then, he too, had to swallow hard.

"What do you mean, howl?"

"Just what I said, Jacob! She howled! Look, I am not about to admit to anyone that I might be in a little over my head here but, damn it, if I don't find out exactly what the hell is going on in Sybil's wild head, it is going to drive me over the edge. I'm going to do an Extraction, Jacob. Two days from now, I have already scheduled us in."

Jacob's gut was now burrowing deeper into itself, huddled there like a small, scared child. Working at the Company was a great gig. Both him and Wilhelm had made their way to the top almost too easily. The benefits of this job were insurmountable, the fame, the attention, the female Consumers that would woo and drool over him. He had no complaints. Extractions, however, were another matter altogether.

He hated being in such close proximity to the uncontrollable insides of a Dreammaker's mind. There was nothing he could ever do to make Extractions more palatable to him. Try as he might, something inside him found them absolutely gory and distasteful. What's more, his role as Extractor made him feel so impotent, just sitting there, having to endure the wild and crazy speech that would come out of all of them. He avoided them as much as he ever could and, as Wilhelm turned around to look at him, he knew what was coming.

"Jacob, I need you to be my partner for it."

To say it straight, all Jacob would have wanted to do at that moment would have been to bolt right out the door, make his way to the Nutrition Center and flirt with one of the many attendants there who were so coquettish with him, pretending that none of this conversation had even occurred. Instead, he bared his teeth, dug his fingers into the seat and said, ¨At what time do you need me?¨

Wilhelm gave the smallest of exhales, an almost imperceptible one, and his shoulders lost their square edge.

¨The appointment is set for eleven in the morning, room A918. Look Jacob, I know you hate these things. Believe me, so do I. I think you should know that Walt sent for me yesterday and told me that he has a watchful eye on Sybil's case. He told me, in so many words, that my job was on the line here and that I had better make up for the havoc that Sybil wreaked on her last two Streams. This Extraction is absolutely necessary, Jacob. There's no one else I would trust to do this with other than you.¨

Jacob nodded his head. He understood the situation perfectly. ¨Eleven it is, brother. I'll see you then.¨

Chapter X

o o o

Sybil was making her way down the corridor again, back to the Beauty Lounge, for her hair appointment. Wilhelm had sent her a message telling her to get ready for an Extraction the next day and a Stream very soon after. He had then scribbled, in tight penmanship, under the typed font, the words, "Your hair is very distasteful these days, please fix it before you come to our appointment."

When she arrived, she found Gretchen smothered in green goo, wearing cucumbers for eyes and having her eyebrows plucked, sitting back placidly on the seat next to where her own hair would be done.

Gretchen was also a Dreammaker. They had met many times before but did not know each other well.

"Sybil, is that you darling?"

How Gretchen could tell it was her, hidden as she was behind the vegetable spectacles, was a mystery.

"Oh sweetie, don't be so surprised," Gretchen said, as if reading Sybil's mind, "It's your smell, dear. I could tell it was you from even before you came in. There is something about your scent honey, unmistakeable, a bit like old gooseberries or fermenting rose vinegar." She smiled and then winced as her Beautician plucked a particularly thick hair from where it was, apparently, not meant to be.

Sybil sat down as her Beautician placed a plastic apron over her chest and shoulders.

"Miss Sybil, Mr. Grim has sent very specific instructions for what he wants us to do to your hair today, Miss. I am sorry, but I am going to have to cut quite a bit off this time."

Sybil tried to smother a whimper but whimpers, as everyone knows, are rascals, and this one popped onto the floor, toppled over the scissor tray, somersaulted into the trash bin and then leaped raucously out the window into an uncertain destiny.

"I'm sorry Miss Sybil, I am just following orders."

As her Beautician began to comb back her hair and spray it with water, Gretchen let a shy grin wriggle its way through her very beautifully built cheekbones, "Maybe," her voice was pregnant with mystery, "maybe you should get your hair dyed red, Sybil, just like Magdalena used to have."

Both Beauticians gasped expressively and then gave each other long looks. But Gretchen's voice, perfectly crafted, dipped in caramel and dusted with sugar, poised itself seductively into her audience's ears and not one of them was able to resist. The Beauticians pretended to make their bodies busy with their tasks, while their attention stayed steady on the conversation that was about to ensue.

"Magdalena?" asked Sybil, taking the bait naively.

"Oh sweet, young Sybil. You don't know about Magdalena, my sweet? You truly do live up to your award's name, 'Essence of Innocence', honey. There's a lot, I guess, that Anne and Bella don't tell you then, I see. Maybe Mr. Grim just doesn't let them. Oh well..." Gretchen's voice faded masterfully into silence, waiting in ambush for Sybil's curiosity to come searching for it.

Sybil squirmed gently in her seat. Unknowingly, Gretchen's voice had taken her by the hand and she was now being led, quite willingly, into winding and uncertain paths.

"Gretchen, no, I've never heard of Magdalena. Do tell me, won't you?"

Gretchen smiled again, even as another rebel hair got plucked away while trying to claim land rights on her side temple, and said, slyly, "Well, if you insist."

She began, "Magdalena was around many, many years ago, Sybil, honey, before any of us were at the Company. She was one of the first Dreammakers and the Director himself was on her case as a Teller. Her Recruiters were never very open about how or where she was found. Similarly to you, actually, she did not have parents or anyone who was taking care of her. Apparently, she too was lying naked, shivering in a corner, when she was finally tracked down and brought in.

"It is said that the whole corridor where she sat in smelled of intoxicating honeysuckle and inebriating lilacs. It is also said that she had a wild and exotic mane on her head, red like the blood of a pomegranate, hirsute like the peel of a rambutan, and untameable like a field of wild Afghan poppies.

"No matter what her Beauticians did for her, that burst of tangles made her look like she was always ablaze.

"The Director was, apparently, extremely taken by her and doused her in extravagant jewelry and clothing. It is said that, one time, he dressed her in a gown made purely of stag beetle shells and made her do her Stream in that outfit.

"But Magdalena was never taken by the expensive clothes and jewelry, or the fancy food and perfumes. She was never moved by any of the gifts that the Director ever gave her, except for one. The strangest of choices, really honey pie, quite bizarre. She apparently loved a small fox pelt that the Director had given her, almost offhandedly. She wore it everywhere, Sybil, everywhere. There are rumors that she would even shower with it and sleep in it. After she passed, when her objects were being raffled off to Consumer fans, that pelt was apparently nothing more than wisps of fur stitched together by thin, decaying string. I never could understand that choice myself. If I had access to the things she was getting, Sybil dear, well I'd be in heaven.

"In any case, Magdalena was, and still is, the biggest hit the Company has ever seen. In a short time, her Stream took over the entire Network. Audiences would pile in every Tuning Day and watch her with their big, wide eyes, watching her every move, listening to every single thing she would say. They drank her up completely. The whole idea of Merchandise began with her: tiny Magdalena dolls, pink T-shirts with her magnificent face plastered all over them, play makeup kits, Magdalena inspired doll houses, tiny Magdalena plastic kitchenettes for young girls to play in… the Consumers could not get enough of her, I tell you. They wanted her to be with them not only through their Stream

Screen but with them all the time, inside their little homes, inside their little kitchens, inside their little bathrooms. Everywhere, Sybil, everywhere.

"This was back in the days when the Director would be seen walking around the Company. People said they had never seen him so happy. Sometimes he would even be spotted skipping, now that's an image, so delighted he was with the success of his protege. But then, trouble started to stir."

The two Beauticians seemed to come in closer, as if Gretchen's voice had fastened itself around them, gently pulling them, luring them closer and deeper into the tale she was telling. Sybil too, had apparently forgotten altogether about the dreadful havoc and disaster that was happening to the top of her head and leaned in, wanting to get as close to the source of the tale as possible.

"Trouble started when Magdalena forgot one of her scripts. It was one of the most iconic Streams she had. It was famously known as Script 37. She had repeated it so many times by then that it was absolutely incomprehensible how she could have completely forgotten the whole ending of it, but so she did. Even worse, the Stream was going on live. Mr. Walt had to practically coax the whole thing out of her as if she were a complete amateur. She barely got through it and, when she was unplugged from the Media Outlet, she apparently went into a long coma that lasted almost seven days."

Gretchen got quiet for a second. Her voice loosened around her listener's ears for a moment as she craned her neck down. When her face came up again, there was something different about her, as if she had looked into an unexpected place and was trying to make sure she still had her footing. After clearing her throat for a moment, she continued, "This is the part of Magdalena's story that I can never fully comprehend, Sybil. The stories that come from those seven days are so wild and difficult to swallow, that a better part of me thinks it's all a bunch of poppycock. It's so beyond reason."

Gretchen shook her head and seemed to find her footing again. A tease of a smile came back to her and, with a tickle, she said, "But it makes the time go by as we sit here in the Beauty Lounge, doesn't it?"

Sybil nodded slowly in agreement and pretended to be nonchalant about what she was hearing. Inside, however, Magdalena's story was like a boa constrictor, slowly wrapping itself around her insides and making it difficult for her to think or breathe anything other than what she was hearing.

"Rumor has it that the Director had Magdalena moved into his own personal apartment, so that he could monitor her at all times. Well, that's what they say. Anyway, he had nurses with her at all times, Beauticians were coming round to take care of her unmoving body and, at nights, she was plugged into a machine to make sure she was still breathing.

"It was the machine that apparently woke the Director up on the seventh day of her convalescence. It was going wild, beeping madly. As if it had gotten the idea that it was trying to make some kind of avant garde musical composition of a sort. Magdalena was huffing and puffing and breathing all kinds of maniacal melodies into that beeping machine and the Director was going insane with the ruckus.

"Then Magdalena woke up, covered in sweat, her eyes popping out of her sockets in hysteric frenzy and this part, well, this part is where I give up all hope of any of this being true. Well, they say that...oh my, I almost can't say this with a straight face it's so funny. They say that, as she came to, she gave out one big, long howl!"

With that, Gretchen let out a loud cackle, more like the strange sound a hyena might make during mating season than a laugh but a laugh nonetheless, while the two Beauticians added their own notes to the chorus, peeping and wheezing in delirious staccatos, while closing their eyes and holding their bellies with their hands as their bodies shook in complete amusement.

The stark contrast of Gretchen and the Beauticians falling apart in laughter versus Sybil's absolute stone-cold silence made for a strange scene. She thought it wisest to pretend to laugh too, so she let out a loud squawk and made as if she too were shaking in merriment when in fact she was shaking for completely other reasons.

Once everyone was down to post-chortle sighs, Sybil said, "What happened after that, Gretchen?"

Gretchen raised an eyebrow and felt short changed with her story. Usually, when she had told the story before, that was the end: the audience was merry, punchline had been served and everyone went about their business as if nothing very relevant had ever truly happened. Here, however, was Sybil in earnestness asking for more, as if what she had already given were not enough, as if her skills were not sufficient for such a pompous little wretch as this so-called Dreammaker star. She felt queasy and wanted to get the green goo off her face as quickly as possible.

"Then? What do you mean, "then" Sybil? That was a good story. Even you can admit that!"

Sybil felt like she was walking onto uncertain territory. She sensed that anything she would say at that moment would be turned against her and, had she been more privy to social mores and correctness, she could have perhaps laughed it off, praised Gretchen and then looked into the mirror to see her new brown bob quiver and wave around her in auburn amusement.

But Sybil was not privy to social mores and correctness. One may blame the fact that she was an orphan, or the fact that she only started being Tuned when she joined the Company or, if one is feeling defiant, one may even blame the Nutrition Center for not giving her a balanced mix of vitamins and minerals. One is free to blame whoever one feels inclined to blame, but the point is that Sybil did not laugh and look at her bob, instead, she said, "Yes, Gretchen, it's a very good story indeed, and I would like to hear the rest of it. What happened after Magdalena woke up howling?"

Gretchen huffed and puffed under her breath. She mumbled something about how she deserved better than this, how she should be pampered more for receiving this sort of treatment, how she would tell on Sybil next time she saw one of the handsome brothers Grim, and as she muttered on, she discovered another part of her voice taking up the thread of where she had left off. Even she was surprised, and listened on intently.

"What happened next, Sybil, is quite shocking. The Director is said to have taken Magdalena in his arms and carried her directly to an Extraction unit. He hooked her up and, without any assistant or anyone else there to help him, he plugged her straight into the Visibility Screen and had a look straight into the images from Magdalena's mind.

"No one has ever heard what it is that he saw in there but what we do know is that that was the day that the Director stopped being seen around the Company. He went into complete isolation in the top floor and barely has any contact with anyone working here, except for his assistant and the occasional Teller or two."

The Beauticians had finished their job at this point and neither of them felt like they wanted to hear the rest of the Dreammakers' conversation. They had had their laughs and neither of them were of the temperament to enjoy the obtuse or the bizarre. They gathered up Gretchen's green goo to add to her Merchandise Beauty Bottles that would be sold later that week and then slowly disappeared into the background, sweeping some invisible dust in the far corners of the Beauty Lounge.

Sybil and Gretchen got closer to each other and, in something close to whispers, Gretchen went on, "Magdalena was taken out of the Extraction unit and moved into one of the secret labs, those that we've only heard about but have never actually seen. Well, apparently they exist and were running in full functioning order because what he did to Magdalena in there is beyond anything I can understand.

"They say that Magdalena was hooked up to a Visibility Screen one more time and then…" Gretchen shuddered audibly, the whole room got colder and the two Beauticians were seen to put both their fingers into their ears and sing the song, "Here we go 'round the mulberry bush…" repeatedly for the next many minutes. "Then, the Director began to dissect her, Sybil. He opened her up. He took her apart. He went through every inch of her body and brain, all the while keeping her hooked up to the Visibility Machine and having her psychic images displayed for him to see.

"She died there, Sybil. She died on that cold, plastic bed, under phosphorescent lights and all those needles poking her and scalpels slicing her. The story the Director told everyone was that Magdalena had passed away during her sleep and that she was resting now very peacefully. The Company organized a funeral like they do for every Dreammaker. He stitched her back up, dressed her in fine linens and drenched her in all kinds of beauty products so she could lay in her casket all pretty and doll-like, so all of her fans could come and say goodbye to her. Her belongings were auctioned off and now she lives like all the rest of them: as a face in a frame in the History Corridor, for us all to look up to and commemorate."

Gretchen could not believe what she had heard herself say. In fact, she did not even know she knew this information until that very moment and, as she slid off the cucumber disks from her eyes, she looked deeply into Sybil's gaze and, in unspoken unison, they both agreed to never mention anything that had happened that day to anyone else. Then they turned back to their respective seats, looked at themselves in their respective mirrors and never spoke to each other again.

Chapter XI

o o o

Bella was holding Sybil's hand as the two of them walked down the carpeted corridor. Anne walked beside them, nodding and smiling at everyone passing by. They were making their way to the Extraction unit A918 and the three of them seemed to be in great spirits. In Anne and Bella's mind, things had now gone completely back to normal. Sybil was taking her medication of her own accord, she was eating the food that the Nutrition Center gave her, and she had been sleeping soundly, with complete Non-mental activity, every night since Bella had found her sweating in bed.

Although Bella had been informing the brothers Grim about Sybil's activities, it was now more a mere protocol and a bit of a nuisance, since everything was back to normal and there had been absolutely no hiccups for almost ten days straight.

As they were making their way through the many maze-like corridors, Bella remembered the first time she and Sybil ever made their way to this wing of the Company.

It had only been about a month since Sybil's arrival, and both of the brothers Grim were ready to bring Sybil in for an Extraction. She could hear her own voice talking gently to the still stick-skinny little brunette that seemed to be ill-fitted to any kind of clothing anyone put on her, but who had become so docile as her days at the Company had gone by.

She could recall herself saying, "Sybil dear, get ready now. You are going to be getting an Extraction today, an absolutely necessary procedure. I know it could be scary at the beginning, there will be a lot around you that will be very unfamiliar but, don't worry, you will have the two most brilliant and wonderful Tellers in the whole Company guiding you the whole way."

Sybil had nodded feebly and Anne then took up the thread of the conversation, "Look Sybil, Extractions are a process that let the Tellers connect to your mind like never before. You will be put to sleep with some very harmless, very gentle medication and then hooked up to the Visibility Screen. As you fall asleep, you will have to find your Bridgepiece, dear, an object that you will carry with you every time you go into an Extraction or a Stream. Once you ring it and the sound is clearly audible to you, you will be taken even deeper into your psychic awareness, to places you never even knew were inside you."

Bella nodded in agreement and then said, "It is utter chaos in there, Sybil. Confusion is rampant anywhere you look. There are monstrosities in there, it is impossible to understand a single thing that is happening and it is so easy, so very easy, to get lost in there. We could never go in there on our own, it would be too dangerous, too risky. Fortunately for us, we have someone who is with us the whole way, someone who will explain everything we are seeing, someone who will guide us and keep us safe the whole way through. The Tellers, Sybil, are our true heroes and we owe everything to them. All our success is due to them. All of the popularity of our Streams is due to their kindness, generosity and superior intelligence. They are the ones who untangle the big mess inside us, dear. And you, you're the luckiest girl. Mr. Wilhelm Grim has taken a liking to you, Sybil…" A small sigh, like a starfish burp, left Bella's chest and floated into one of the vents on the corridor walls, making its way through the winding insides of the great Company building, leaving through a crack in the wall and then mingling with the great gaseous beyond.

Anne then continued, "It is then the job of the Tellers to take our Weaves and make smart, beautiful scripts for us that we can then tell on our Streams for our dear, loyal Consumers to listen to. If it weren't for the Tellers, Sybil, we would have nothing to give our dear audience, we would be utterly useless, fit for nothing. Our Weaves are so incomprehensible, so mixed with utter nonsense. Our Tellers clean everything up for us, allow us to make sense, ensure that what we share on our Channel is Good and Right for everyone watching. It is an incredible system, Sybil. And now you're a lucky, lucky girl to be part of this wonderful, beautiful Company. You should thank your stars you are here and not back in that alley, honey. Had it not been for the Director and his Recruiters, Sybil, you would be absolutely lost, hungry, alone, making absolutely no sense, serving no one. I am so happy for you. Your whole life has changed now and, just like the rest of the Dreammakers here, we owe it to the Company to serve dutifully, to be loyal, to always be Good. This is the first of your Extractions, darling, so make sure you do it well. Make sure to listen to everything Mr. Grim tells you. And, when you get your script back, make sure to memorize it immediately. You want to make a very good first impression."

Anne stopped speaking as they arrived to the Extraction unit door and then knocked to let the Grim brothers know that Sybil had arrived.

In an exact replica of those events that had happened years past, Anne again knocked on the door of the A918 unit. Contrary to their first visit, the Grim brothers did not greet them warmly, beaming as they offered their guests licorice sticks and candy canes dipped in caramelized orange liquor. This time, the two men opened the door tensely and forced themselves into an extremely awkward smile that was not becoming of either of them. There were no treats, no niceties exchanged. Sybil was asked to make her way to the plastic bed in the middle of the room and both Anne and Bella were quickly shooed away.

The two of them gave Sybil one last squeeze of her hands and then left, down the corridor, back the way they had come, Bella slightly ahead while Anne followed suit, a little step behind her the whole way.

Sybil was given the customary glass of sparkling water along with the medication that made her feel drowsy almost instantly. Her shoes off and her head nuzzled into the head cradle behind her, both her eyelids began to get heavier and heavier, until she lay there, eyes completely closed, senses completely turned inwardly and the familiar feeling of her body falling down into an incomprehensible vacuum taking her over completely.

Chapter XII

o o o

Bramble. *I am in a thicket of wild rose bushes and honey locust bark. Wherever I move, my body is pierced by thorns. My movements are tense, calculated, rigid. The space around me defends itself against my presence and I slowly become more entangled in its web of bristles. I hear myself breathing, a rickety breath, as if the air inside me were also being pricked and stung.*

In the distance I hear the sound of running water and, calmed by it, I turn my eyes to find the source. Golden light, like a shimmering shower of honey-dipped scales, fills the bushes I am currently in. My body becomes silky, like a velvet worm, and I slowly drip down the edges of each aggressive edge I was locked in and land on the soft dirt beneath me.

My nostrils are filled with the smell of loving mud. I am close to the ground and make my way forward, deeper into the thicket of the glade I am now in.

The liquid nature of night is condensing onto pine needles and oak leaves around me. I am showered in gentle sprinkles of midnight dew as the sound of my body crossing this green landscape adds its note into the nocturnal symphony that emerges from every corner of this living, luminous domain.

My body has become accustomed to the air around me. Between my skin and the cool night air there is the thinnest of boundaries. My nose has become acutely intelligent. I can smell the live bodies of crickets, voles and caterpillars around me, the very movement of the blood through their veins tickling the insides of my nose.

I am ravenous in a way I have never known before. My hunger yowls through my marrow and my spine articulates itself in an omnivorous dance, weaving its way silently through the thicket. I am all instinct. My rational mind has quieted to a lull and my senses are wired, exalted, amplified, able to encompass the whole bush around me.

I make my way into the mossy wetness of a giant pine tree. One of its many cones creaks under the weight of my body as I walk by and, in an instant, every hair on my body is attuned to the minutiae of this sound crackling through the primeval nightscape. The forest is alive and I know its song, it has been humming itself silently within me all along.

So intoxicated am I that every bone in my body begins to sing the song of the evening sparrow, the melody of the midnight owl, the notes of the nocturnal river rock, the arpeggios of the most ancient of soils. I am pure resonance.

As my ears drink in the ensemble of life around me, from afar, I hear a sound that stands out in its unique, almost dissonant nature.

My soft body makes its way to the edge of the woods and, through the dim lighting of moonbeams, I spot the large, strong body of a man.

He is carrying the dead body of a deer over his shoulder and his footsteps ripple through the earth beneath him. His body has a powerful and clumsy weight to it, completely unaware of the space he inhabits, unable to hear the delicate death of the twigs beneath him, ferocious in his solidity.

I watch him from a distance as he makes his way into a cold stone hut and, when he has gone inside, I come closer, peeking through the window, watching him light his fireplace and begin to cut through the large thighs of the carcass that lays on his round, wooden table.

I can smell the insides of his hut. Everything is covered in the scent of guts and dead hide. The smell undulates towards me, caressing me, inviting me into a seductive dance, smiling and beckoning me to come closer.

I watch the man move in his intelligent and artful motions, knife and hand seemingly one, and my sinews sigh and moan as his blade makes its way through the thick layers of flesh. His knife plunges deeper into the insides of the still warm body and his hand reaches in, searching, caressing, stroking the red and pink tissues until he reaches his goal. He pulls and tugs articulately, an artist at his craft, and slowly, so slowly, hand covered in blood, he pulls out the beast's heart.

My own heart falters for a moment, as if it were an amateur ballroom dancer, throbbing and groaning vehemently as it witnesses all of this happening before it. Suddenly, my own frame shakes in longing and I gaze upon the man's viscous hands and his rough mouth, and delicately ache to be his prey, to give myself in endless generosity, to be eaten in meticulous gruffness, to live inside his digestive juices.

As if my thoughts had been spoken out loud, I watch the man stop for a moment and raise his head, listening intently. The night has become as dark as the center of a black radish and the light from his fire blinds him to the view outside his window. However, he peers out, hunter eyes piercing the window that keeps us apart, and he clasps the very center of my own wild pupil.

I become liquid, luminescent, the very essence of the forest around me. He becomes immovable solidity. In my mouth, I taste the strange flavor of his flesh grinding against my gums and teeth, and my own body mixing in his saliva, quietly becoming soft in the rough textures of his thick tongue and hard dentition. We devour each other into the silent night, until the only thing left between us is the gentle hum and heat of the crackling fire and the redolent chorus of crickets at dawn.

Chapter XIII

o o o

Wilhelm's spine wheezed as Jacob shivered, covered in cold sweat. Neither of them spoke or even looked at each other. Something inside them trembled acutely. Silence reigned as the Visibility Screen turned dark. They could not imagine a single word being welcomed into the strange and almost thick space they were inhabiting.

Sybil lay on the bed, radiantly beaming, almost glowing, eyes still closed as the medication began to wear off.

As she began to regain consciousness, she tenderly stretched her long arms over her head, like a happy tigress after a nap in the sun and then opened her eyes, lazily looking out at the white walls of the unit where she lay.

She turned her head to find her Tellers white-faced and stunned. Being used to their very correct behavior and their ability to always be in control of any situation, Sybil felt uncomfortable and quickly disconnected herself from the many wires that were attached to the various points on her head.

"Is...is...is everything all right?" She ventured to ask.

She was met with the same stony silence. Confused as she was, upon reprising the situation, she decided to escort herself to the door and quietly leave.

For Sybil, Extractions were always her favorite part of her time at the Company. Although she could never remember what exactly happened during any of them, she always woke up feeling refreshed and at ease with herself. She had hoped to open her eyes to the approving gaze of the brothers Grim. She had hoped to receive praise as she had many times before. She had hoped to look up at them and feel like she had done a Good Job. Their reaction, however, had left her bewildered. She made her way down the corridor, back to her chambers, and lay there for a time, staring up at the ceiling and pondering many unanswered questions.

Meanwhile, back at unit A918, the brothers finally broke their silence in awkward throat clearing, nose blowing and cumbrous fiddling around with their attire.

"I...well that was...I think that..." Jacob's attempts at a sentence left vocabulary nodding its head in shameful disapproval.

Some more moments of silence passed, until Wilhelm made his own courageous attempt at emitting speech, "That was...well...that was worse than I thought."

"Yes, brother. I agree." Vocabulary, although underwhelmed by Jacob's new attempt, decided to give him a second chance.

Wilhelm tapped at the Visibility Screen, scrolling through the images they had both just witnessed and sighed loudly.

"I can't work with this, Jacob. I simply can't. We have to erase it, pretend it never happened. We'll have to release another Stream, give her another script, make her forget any of this ever even occurred."

Jacob shuddered again as a memory of what he had just seen waltzed its way through the corridors of his own shocked mind.

"She has taken her medication, Jacob. She has been eating correctly, exercising, going to her Beauty appointments. Bella and Anne are with her every moment of every day. There is not a single minute where she has been left on her own. I don't understand. I just can't comprehend where she would get this kind of shit from. She's irremediable." A pause, a hard swallow. "I am at my wit's end."

Jacob looked down at the floor, as if trying to find an answer between the perfectly laid tiles. Finding nothing there, he asked, "Wilhelm, what about Walt? Are you going to tell him about this?"

Wilhelm looked at Jacob for a moment and then turned his gaze back to the empty space of the white walls that surrounded him. Suddenly, the room seemed incredibly small. He loosened his tie and cracked his knuckles nervously.

"I see no other choice. I could not hide something like this without being caught sooner or later. Besides, he's been watching our every move. There is nothing I can do with this, Jacob. You know I'm right, you watched it too. Truly. How could I clean this up? Impossible. It is absolute profanity from beginning to end. I know the Director must have dealt with stuff like this back at the very beginning, when no one had ever been Tuned, when things were absolutely profane and people had access to every part of themselves. But that was so incredibly long ago, back when he was still cleaning all of this up. But look how far we've come along. We have not seen a Dreammaker's Extraction come even close to anything like this in years. Years! The stuff we deal with is fluff, Jacob. Everyone that comes here is so tidy, so close to Rightness and Goodness. Their Extractions barely have any content to them at all. We barely even have to modify things much. You know I'm right. But this. I don't even know what to say about what we just saw. I have never in my life been even remotely close to anything as absolutely insane, base and disgusting as what I just witnessed this evening. I can't believe I was made to watch the ludicrous mess that that woman holds inside her. Jacob, I, I can't imagine myself working with her ever again. It would break me, I am embarrassed to admit it but it's just beyond me at this point."

Silence walked into the room again and sat down between the two men, its large and rotund shape pressing up against their manly frames.

It was Jacob who spoke up this time, "Wilhelm, what if…what if we tried that old script, the script that was taken off the air back in Walt's early days? You know, the script that was once incredibly famous…The one Magdalena told…It could work."

Wilhelm's gaze came up and, looking straight at his brother, his eyes widened and, for a moment, he seemed to drop his gloom.

Script 37. Yes, that was a brilliant idea. For a moment, Wilhelm's hopes came back to life. Script 37 had so many of the elements that they had just witnessed. Sybil could be easily fooled. Not only that, they could use the Script to bring her back to her senses. Modify it a bit to give her a deep lesson in Morality. Perhaps even ride on the Script's old popularity. Perhaps regain the audience they had lost. Maybe even skyrocket to the top! Yes, yes. The Script! It was a brilliant idea.

As Wilhelm began to regain the color in his cheeks, Jacob looked at his watch and realized he was late for an appointment. He gathered his belongings, put on his coat and, as he made his way to the door, turned around and, without looking in any particular direction, said, "Those images are going to haunt me for the rest of my life, brother."

Chapter XIV

o o o

Sybil lay in a tub of warm oat milk. Anne was busily humming and bustling around the room, interrupting her songs every so often with quiet exclamations and expressions of surprise and delight. Bella sat behind the tub, gently combing the short bob that now rested, like a curled up badger, at the top of Sybil's head.

¨I can't believe you got an invitation to visit the Director himself, Sybil,¨ said Bella, as the wooden comb made its way through the brown tresses which, even at this short length, still managed to run amok and go every which way.

¨I know, I am very surprised too. When I received the invitation, I thought it must have been a mistake, some kind of administrative error.¨

But no, it had not been a mistake. The envelope was very much intended for Sybil and had arrived earlier that day, to her very chambers, smelling of cotton candy and confectioner sugar. It had been hand-written in elegant, black ink. The words swirled on the silver paper they were written on, making it appear as if the font itself were trying to hypnotize its reader into an intoxicated stupor.

Along with the invitation, there had come a small hand woven basket made of sophisticated fibers that could not hide the fact that they came from a far off homeland and, inside it, were twelve perfectly made gingerbread men, each one dotted with expertly drawn green and blue icing for their tiny sugar suits and meticulously placed red and white candy drops for their eyes and mouths.

Sybil had placed the gingerbread men on a small table for her friends to enjoy. Bella and Anne had happily bitten into them, nodding and munching, as tiny crumbs fell to the floor, but Sybil could not seem to find the will or wish to tuck into any of these tiny baked bodies and so had contented herself with watching her friends enjoy the gift. Until now, the Director had only sent her expensive gifts and jewelry. She had been told that this was not common at all but she never made much of it. This invitation, however, was completely unexpected and she was not quite sure what to make of it.

Her meeting with the Director was scheduled for that evening and Anne and Bella had insisted on coming over to help her get ready.

As soon as she was out of the bath, they powdered her in conch shell talc, painted her eyelids in shades of ruby and crimson hues, rouged her cheeks with zinnia dust, painted her lips with the juices of a mature beet, and dressed her in the elegant folds of a gown made solely of anemone and aster petals.

As Bella gave the look her finishing touches, a knock came at the door and a thinly framed assistant announced that she was there to escort Miss Sybil to the Director's office.

Chapter XV

o o o

The corridors transformed from the grey walls and carpets that Sybil was familiar with to a lush maze of sleek silver panels and extravagant tapestries.

After quite a long journey, the thin assistant came to a door, knocked gently, turned to Sybil, nodded, and left silently back from where they had just come.

"Come in." The voice came from inside. A warm voice, like taffy it was, and it beckoned Sybil in immediately.

The room felt expensive. The very air was laden with luxury. Even in her gown and makeup, Sybil felt out of place, as if she did not belong in the richness of the environment.

She stood at the doorway, beholding the entirety of the room decorated in lavish ornaments, when she heard the same voice come closer to her and say, "Come in, child. Come in. I've been expecting you."

The voice's owner came forward and was lit by the light coming from the large chandelier that hung imperiously from the ceiling. The light was warm, it spilled down like expensive honey and made the speaker appear to be bathed in liquid gold.

Sybil took a step forward and got a closer look at the man that was standing before her. He exuded a calm and confident air about him. The scent of macaroons and freshly made merengue emerged from the seams of his well-fitted suit. His body was tall and slightly rounded at the edges and a large, bushy beard, which reminded Sybil of a baby seal's fur, so soft and bushy it was, grew out of his open and smiling face. For no clear reason, Sybil felt surprised at her interlocutor's shape and form. Although The Director's face appeared in many commercials, she had not been sure what to expect. Sybil was confused with the presence of the completely friendly and warm person that stood before her.

His voice rippled through her observations and invited her to sit down on the plush sofa that he was pointing at with his large and pudgy hands.

She sat down, smoothing out the crimson petals under her thighs.

"May I offer you something to drink, dear one? Apple juice? Grape extract? Perhaps a glass of milk?"

Sybil nodded, seemingly not hearing that she had to make a choice and instead looked down at the animal crackers that lay in a bowl in the center of the coffee table before her.

"A glass of milk it is." The Director handed her a tall glass of the white liquid and proceeded to sit on the sofa opposite her.

"Well now, Sybil dear, I hear that you have been well taken care of by Miss Bella and Mrs. Anne. Kind and noble creatures they are. I hope you have found their company to your liking."

Sybil sat and listened to the baritone voice emerge from the wide and whisker-laden mouth. She wondered what to respond and, finding that her voice had decided to take a leave of absence, simply nodded, over and over again, looking, to be quite honest, slightly foolish as she did so.

"Well, we could only pick the gentlest and sweetest to accompany someone such as yourself during your stay here at the Company. I am pleased to hear that you spend much of your time with them and that they have been very helpful throughout your whole process and training here. Wonderful news that is. I am very pleased."

Sybil continued to sit in silence and nod. Even the milk in her glass felt a twinge embarrassed for her.

¨You've had wonderful ratings now, haven't you. The best show airing on any of our Channels, most audience views, you've been winning Awards… You are quite the success now, aren't you, darling?¨

At the risk of monotony, indeed, Sybil nodded again.

The Director reached down into the cookie-filled bowl, pulled out one of the many baked shapes from within it, and proceeded to munch down on the miniature shape of a chimpanzee.

¨Oh my, that reminds me, Sybil. You haven't met Pupi. How could I be so neglectful! Goodness me. You are going to love him. Pupi! Pupi!¨

The Director's voice traveled through the spacious expanse of the luscious room and, from behind a curtain, some movement was heard.

¨Pupi, come here. Don't be bashful now. Let Miss Sybil see you.¨

Sybil looked over and, emerging from the velvety folds, came a small mochaccino monkey, dressed in a fitted tuxedo, with small, angular and flawlessly shined shoes and the smallest of bowties adorning his flawlessly groomed body. He was standing perfectly straight. His tail had been cut off and, had it not been for his furry face, one could have mistaken him for being a very short, well-dressed, middle aged man.

"Pupi, come here."

The small monkey made his way towards the sofa, his tiny shoes giving him an awkward gate and, when he had come quite close to Sybil, he extended his hand out in greeting. Sybil was confused again and, deeming it unwise to simply nod for the fourth time in a row, extended her own hand in response.

As they shook hands, the Director clapped his hands in joyful exultation.

"I knew the two of you would get along handsomely."

Pupi took his hand back and proceeded to take a seat next to Sybil. Sitting there, in the middle of that large, mustard-colored couch made him look even smaller.

"Pupi has been with me his whole life," said the Director. "You should have seen him when he arrived, Sybil. You would not be able to recognize him for what he is today. He was so unkept, covered in ticks and fleas, he had mange and bit anyone who came close to him. He was a complete and utter rascal, almost impossible to make behave. But I took pity on the poor creature. I'm like that, you know. I could not bear to watch him suffer, so uncouth he was, so far from propriety and the ways of civilization. It took me a long time, but it was worth it. And now look at him. He is a living example of the reformatory force that some good manners and care can do for anyone. It's about finding and focusing on someone's potential and then, dedication, constant and pure dedication, and never giving up. Love can cure anyone, Sybil. I know that for a fact."

Sybil looked over at Pupi, who was now eating, in the dandiest of fashions and with his tiny pinky finger shooting straight up into the air, one of the cookies (another baked chimpanzee, actually) from the bowl and wiping the crumbs that fell on his clean suit with a small, embroidered handkerchief that he pulled out from his coat pocket.

The Director regarded him too and clasped both his hands over the roundness of his belly and smiled, satisfied and content.

After a moment of silence, the Director continued speaking, "Now, Sybil, I can only imagine you may be wondering why I have called you in this evening."

Sybil, sitting next to the very formal Pupi, decided that she needed to up her game, nodding could only get you so far, and went for a, "Yes…yes, sir." Pupi shot her a sideways glance, feeling quite superior to her for a moment.

"Yes, good question, my child. I have been following your case quite closely, Sybil. Ever since you arrived. Well, indeed, before that even. I've known about you for a very long time. I always make a note to keep a close eye on those poor souls that don't have the same good fortune as any of our other good Consumers. I know you did not have the wonderful opportunity to attend too many Tunings before you came to us and I am well aware of your status as an orphan."

At the mention about details of her past, Sybil looked down and pretended to smooth out some wrinkles in her dress. Although her life before the Company was not often brought up, whenever it was, whoever seemed to be speaking about it always made it appear like it was an undesirable thing to have lingering around her. She had become used to this approach to relating to herself and assumed it was expected of her to feel ashamed. So she did what she had always done, looked away and fidgeted with an innocent bystander object.

The Director reached for a remote control that he then pointed at a screen that sat majestically on the wall beside them. There was nothing to be seen for a moment but then, as clear as day, an image appeared. It was a short clip, in black and white.

"Know who that is, dear?"

It took her a moment to recognize her own self in there. She was so different, almost unrecognizable. She was laying on the side of an alley, huddled in a small, fetal ball, covered in a black plastic bag. She lay there, shuddering, her hair in a shambles all around her, making her look like a barbecued medusa.

The clip was paused at that moment but, as the Director pressed another button, the clip fast forwarded, but the image did not change.

"You were huddled there for days, Sybil. I know, I watched you."

Then the clip changed. Sybil still lay on her side but, from somewhere behind the camera angle, three men dressed in black suits appeared and placed her on a stretcher. Her body remained in the fetal position as the three men slowly carried her out of screen shot and, as she remembered it now, into an ambulance straight to the Company.

"That's when you came to us. And that is when your life changed. Remember the first time you ate warm soup, my little one? I remember. Your face lit up and there was finally some color in your sweet little cheeks. Your bones stopped showing after some time with us and you started eating correctly. You had manners. You were eating with cutlery and at the table, instead of those strange ways you had before, eating with your hands and dribbling all over the place."

Sybil did remember. She was bombarded for a moment with the image of herself sitting at one of the tables at the Nutrition Center, the first time she had been invited to eat with the other Dreammakers and how she had felt like everyone was watching her and how, when she picked up the spoon and had a dainty sip of the stew before her, Anne had beamed and she had felt so happy, so approved of, so like she belonged.

"Yes, yes, darling. You had quite the process at the beginning but your progress was astounding. Our Tellers and Beauticians were all deeply impressed by your transformation. You surprised us all. Even me."

The Director nodded back at the screen and new images now appeared: Sybil getting her hair done for the first time; Sybil starting her fitness program with her personal trainer; Sybil doing jumping jacks in her pink leotard; Sybil fitting into her first gown; Sybil meeting Mr. Wilhelm and Mr. Jacob for the first time; Sybil after her first Stream; Sybil walking into her chamber with Anne and Bella by her side, the three of them smiling. This last frame was paused and then a close up of her beaming face filled the screen.

"You see now, my puppet. You have been so cherished and loved by all of us here at the Company. You can see for yourself how far you have come. You can't forget that now, can you? I knew from the first time I saw you that you were special. That you had that spark that we are always looking for. I send Recruiters out into our Capital's streets all the time, always looking, searching for young girls that have the gift, always trying to find fresh and new talent. They find many girls, Sybil. But no one, no one, compares to you. You are special, Sybil. So special."

The Director was looking straight at Sybil now. His eyes were warm and full of an enchanting charisma that left her defenseless before their safe shores. She watched herself want to curl up inside the Director's gentle gaze, want to lay her head on the warm lap of his pupils. She wanted this moment to last forever, to feel him looking at her, and only her.

It was Pupi's hand, reaching into the cookie bowl, that broke the spell. This time, he was munching on a crocodile, and the tiny handkerchief was wiping off the evidence.

The Director blinked and then looked back at the screen. Sybil secretly cursed the tiny monkey next to her.

"Now Sybil. I have heard from Mr. Wilhelm that things have been a little, how shall I say it, turbulent for a while."

Sybil found herself going red in the face. Her cheeks were warm and flushed and her palms became wet with sweat. She found her voice galloping back from wherever it had gone off on vacation and, in an almost manic frenzy she said, "No! No. I am back to normal now, Sir. We just had a small hiccup for a little while but I am back. I am stable. I am fine now, Mr. Director, Sir. I am taking my medication, going for my jogs, eating at my hours. I even got my hair cut just like Mr. Grim asked me to, Sir." And she shook her head from side to side, trying to prove her point as the bob moved in uniform swooshes to and fro.

"Yes, yes, I see, my girl, my little puppet."

The Director brought his briefcase from under the coffee table, opened it and pulled out a file. As he flipped through the pages, he made an inaudible sigh.

"Yes, I see that what you are saying is all true, Sybil. I have it in our records. Everything meticulously done, completed in excellent form. You are a model of perfect behavior." Sybil sat up a little straighter and now it was she who shot Pupi a sideways glance, which he attempted to ignore by fidgeting with the chain on his tiny hand watch.

"There is a note here, however," Sybil's posture shrunk, she found her stomach tightening. Pupi was now paying full attention, "Mr. Wilhelm has quite a few notes here about your Extraction last evening."

Sybil was genuinely shocked. "My...my Extraction, Sir? Did I not do well? I...I tried my best. I wanted to make the Company proud. I...I thought I had..." Sybil continued stammering inaudibly.

"Now, now, don't you fret, my dear. Let's just go over anything that you remember from your experience."

In all her time at the Company, Sybil had never been asked to remember an Extraction. In fact, she had been adamantly told to actively try and forget anything that happened there, to simply trust the Tellers to process what she had delivered and learn her script as quickly as possible.

Now, however, she was recalling the Director's gaze from a moment ago, the feeling of being someone who could do something Right and Pleasing, and was determined to try her best to do as she was told.

She furrowed her brow and pressed her eyelids closed. Her mouth got tight and, from somewhere deep inside her mind, she tried to bring forth anything, even the smallest of memories but, as she emerged from that cavernous darkness, she came back empty handed.

"I am sorry, Sir. I can't remember a thing."

The Director closed the folder, making a clapping sound that shocked Pupi and made him reconsider reaching out for a third cookie.

"Very good. Very good." The Director's voice was fuller now, it puffed up and rang through the walls of the room where the three of them sat.

"Now Sybil, I want to take you through a little journey with me. Look over here." As he said that, he again pointed the remote control to the screen and a whole new set of images came to the fore.

The images were also in black and white and flipped through different scenes every couple of seconds. The first clip to appear was of the entrance to the Company. It was a busy street, full of Consumers walking busily to and fro, briefcases in hand, a gentle mist in the air. The next image was from the inside of one the many office buildings that surrounded them. It was a large room, filled with cubicles, where more Consumers sat and worked in front of computer screens, diligently typing on their keyboards. The next scene was an aisle at the Refreshment Center. There were tiers of perfectly packaged packets of Morning Munch, where a group of children with their perfectly dressed mothers were walking, picking a pair of their favorite meals and making their way to the cash register. The next scene was of the interior of one of the many Consumer homes. In this one, Consumer X0720 was shown snoring, draped over his very used sofa, his Stream Screen still on and in full technicolor splendor and, before the Director made to turn off the visuals, was heard audibly farting and waking up, grunting and looking around in quizzical confusion.

The screen went black again and the Director turned toward Sybil.

"These, my young girl, are the people we serve. These dedicated and noble creatures are the cream of the crop of civilization. Their manners and etiquette are worthy of great praise. Their morals are unequaled. Their dedication to making this society a place where everything is working in harmony is unparalleled. They are exquisite, our Consumers are, Sybil, quite exquisite."

Pupi made a strange sound. It remains unclear if he was stifling a snicker or, if in between the screen being on and the Director's words, he had managed to take another cookie and had been choking slightly on its dryness.

In any case, the Director threw him a disapproving glance and Pupi swallowed hard, falling back into silence and sinking a little deeper into the furniture beneath him.

"As I was saying, before being rudely interrupted," one more penetrating glance was shot and Pupi was pinned to the upholstery. "These Consumers are what keep this Company going, always trying to improve, always innovating, always staying at the top of our game."

Sybil was listening intently, taken in by the Director's words, beginning to feel proud of what she belonged to, having a warm feeling invade her spine and, for the first time in a very long time, even relaxing a little. She felt safe swimming in the warmth of the Director's voice. She imagined herself sun bathing at the shores of his oceanic timbre and, just as she was about to fully dive into what she had just heard, she was brought back into the room by the sudden, almost brutal, change in the Director's tone.

He had stood up, his hands clasped tightly together behind his back, making his previously warm and slightly reddish hands turn into a little army of white knuckles, like an albino centipede, ready for battle.

Sybil was unsure if, during her daydream, she had accidentally knocked something over, or if Pupi had lost all control and had stifled another snicker, or had perhaps tried to devour yet another cookie. It was unclear to her. Unsure of what had given rise to the sudden change, she sat back and held her breath as she watched the Director pace back and forth before her.

It was a grumble under his breath that broke the dam of silence into which the Director had retreated as he paced back and forth. The grumble turned into a huff and the huff turned into his fist slamming against the coffee table.

Both Pupi and Sybil jumped a little out of their seats, gulped, and then remained wide eyed and stunned, watching the Director's every move.

His face had turned crimson, as if he too had decided to sunbathe on that beach next to Sybil but had neglected to wear sunscreen, stayed out for too long and was now more like a crustacean, the sunburn having fried him a little too much.

From his once articulate mouth, all that emerged now was incomprehensible muttering and the occasional grunt.

Although still confused and unsure of what had just happened, she decided to venture, in the meekest of voices, the words, ¨S..Sir…are you…are you OK?¨

The Director looked up and, where there once had been the softest of gazes, there was now steely coldness that made Sybil shudder and pull the folds of her dress closer to her.

¨Ok? Sybil, I don't think you understand the gravity of this situation in the slightest.¨

Sybil had to agree. Indeed not only did she not understand the gravity of the situation, she actually felt like she had lost all contact with ground control and was now floating in space, in gravity-less confusion and quite unsure of how she had gotten there in the first place.

It was a knock on the door that momentarily interrupted the tension in the room.

The Director looked up, seemingly confused for a moment, and then the thin-framed woman from before walked daintily into the room and said, "Sir, your evening paper has arrived."

She held in her hands a newspaper, which she was now placing on one of the many elegant desks that adorned the room and then turned to face the Director with a magnificently curated smile on her very well made up face.

"Alexa...Alexa, yes. How could I forget, yes of course. My evening paper. Thank you."

"Will you be needing anything else, Sir?"

"No, no thank you Alexa. Not for now. You are free to go."

Alexa gave a small curtsy, nodded cordially at Sybil and Pupi and made her way back out the large doors.

The Director stood in the middle of the room, proceeded to readjust his suit and then walked back to the sofa. He regarded Sybil again. She sat there, her face expressionless, waiting to see what would happen next.

The Director cleared his throat, seemed to reassess his tactics and, in a warmer tone said, "Sybil dear, do you know anything about the history of this Company?"

Sybil shook her head from side to side, the bob moving along in perfectly choreographed lateral swooshes.

"Let me enlighten you on the matter then." The Director readjusted himself in his seat and began, "Many years ago, this society lay in complete havoc. People ran amok, completely dominated by their selfish desires, their personal confusion, and the great ignorance that polluted their minds. It was a sad, sad world that one, Sybil. People had no clue how to lead a decent existence, had no idea how to live a meaningful life. They were so child-like in all of their decisions. Everywhere you looked, these people were suffering. And the worst part of it all is that it was all their own doing. They had so much freedom, so many choices, such great potential, but such little direction, such little capacity to know how to guide their lives into anything worthwhile. It was awful, truly a living hell.

"I knew, even as a child, that I was different, that there was something fundamentally distinct about my outlook on life than to anyone else I knew. I looked out at this world and saw immense sorrow and my heart was moved. I wanted to do something for the people of this world. I wanted to make my life a living masterpiece of compassion and love. And so I began a journey that, in its initial stages, I could not conceive would become what it is today.

"I took a deep interest in people. I listened, I cared. I spent days and days talking to anyone who would tell me their life's story. And after a long time, amidst thousands of tales, thousands of variations on the colors and tones of the storyline, I came to a conclusion: even though everyone's story seemed unique on the outside, there was one common thread among all of them."

The Director paused for dramatic effect. Sybil leaned in a little closer, despite still being a little unsure about what the Director would do next. He then said, "Do you know what that is?"

Both Pupi and Sybil shook their heads.

"Fear. Fear was the common factor among every single person I spoke to. They were terrified of themselves, Sybil. Absolutely scared to death of what lay inside them. And, to be honest, after speaking to so many of them, I understand why. No wonder this society was such an utter incomprehensible mess. It was laid on faulty foundation, completely ignoring what lay at its core, what was rotten at the root.

¨Well, I had done enough research at that point to know that I had to take action. It was not enough to know the problem, it was time to do something about it. Now that I had spent so much time doing such extensive research, I had become somewhat of an authority on human nature. At that point, I needed only to look at someone for a moment to know what troubled them, to understand what lay deep within them that so anguished them and would not let them rest at night. I knew things about people that none of them knew, the deep dark secrets, the part that lay in the shadow.

¨So I began this Company. Back then it was just myself, none of this infrastructure was around. It was just me, in a room with one chair, one bed, and a tiny screen that I would hook people up to so as to be able to see the images they saw in their minds.

¨I invited people to come to my office and I would hook them up to the various wires and ask them to lay down on the bed. I would ask them to breathe for some time and listen to my voice and, after a while, they would forget their troubles and relax deeply. They would fall asleep and, once they did, I would ask them about their lives.

¨It is amazing what people will tell you when they are asleep. Truly astounding. There are so many deep, dark caverns inside our mind, Sybil, places we would never dare go to if we were awake and conscious. But in the sleep state, everything is available.

"While these people slept, I listened. And then discovered that I could actually guide them. I could guide them through their murky mental labyrinths and, once I started doing this, people began to improve. Sybil, I was helping them! Truly helping them. One after another, people would leave my office clearer, lighter, able to live productive and happy lives. I was able to clean up their inner confusion. I was able to help them understand themselves.

"I realized that I had to grow, that this technology had to expand. So I began to charge and spread the word and, soon enough, people were lining up at my door by the dozens. I used the money that people paid me to buy the building you are now sitting in. However, I soon began to face the problem of not being able to attend my growing number of patients.

"I realized I would have to train someone else to help me. This, however, was a harder hurdle than anything else I had had to face before. I tried training a young man but soon realized my effort was completely in vain. He had too many ideas of his own, too much inner confusion. It was a complete disaster. I left him alone with a patient and the result was catastrophic. It was like giving a free access pass to a small child into another small child's playground. He could not remotely understand the inner trappings of their mind and the patient was left in worse state than when they had come in.

"The solution dawned on me then that I needed to train this man during his sleep. I guided him as he lay in my office, into the firm territory of nobility and service. I retrained his thoughts, I let him learn the deepest meanings of what is Right and what is Wrong. I tuned him, carefully and with dedication, like a perfect instrument. After a very short time, the young man that then stood before me was a model of perfection. He was living proof that my work was of great meaning, that it could change a person forever.

"We began our work together. He excelled and performed wonderfully. I soon realized I would need more assistants, and so began the process of training more young men. Soon I had a small army of what you now know as Tellers at my command. Together we worked on endless cases and, slowly but surely, we saw the world before us transform completely.

"Society became a word to be proud of, a privilege to belong to. Everyone was Good, not superficially, Sybil. No, to the core. True Harmony became a way of living.

"After many years of my diligent work, I realized I could make my work even more efficient and began the Streaming Service that you are now so familiar with. In this way, we would not have to attend one person at a time, instead, we could work with thousands of people at a time, Tuning them, perfecting them, turning each and every one of them into Model Citizens.

"Hiccups still occurred in these early days. From time to time, someone would act out, someone would become confused, experience fear, do something Wrong. Again, through active diligence, I figured out a way to prevent this from ever happening again.

"The time for Recruiters came, a wonderful and beautiful service. I began monitoring every member of our society closely to recognize any potential outburst. It was always young women. Men became immune to any kind of psychic turbulence. But our young women, sweet, innocent and weaker creatures, they are the ones who are most prone to these undesirable experiences. In another brilliant move, we began to bring these young women into the Company before a problem would even arise and, by extracting the psychic mess that lay within them, we would then iron out any confusion she might still have and then, in an even more innovative solution, we began Streaming these young women, telling a story and sharing what they had just healed on Screens all over the nation and, voila, a national vaccine. No one would ever have to go through the inner turmoil that these young women had the potential to experience because we got to the problem before it even arose. National psychic inoculation! Brilliant!"

The Director's voice had returned to its once soft tones and he sat back in his sofa, quite content, enamored by everything he had just said.

"Beautiful, isn't it Sybil? Just absolutely beautiful. A masterpiece, I would even dare say. I look out my window at this creation and behold utter majesty. Everything running perfectly, everyone doing their best. Truly a paradise."

The Director was indeed looking out the window, enchanted and enthralled, forgetting Sybil and Pupi's presence all together.

Sybil did not know if it would be right for her to interrupt the Director's reverie and, in the uncertainty, she fidgeted slightly, which caused the sofa beneath her to creak and pull the Director right back into the room and look straight into Sybil's uncomfortable face.

With his eyes steadily set on Sybil, the Director began turning crimson again, the white knuckles came back to the party and, standing up furiously, he exclaimed, "But you! You! You absolute freak of nature. You unethical creature of absolute inadequacy. You uncouth woman. You are a disgrace to all that is Proper, Good and Correct!"

Sybil's legs started to tremble, followed soon by her teeth and then the white in her eyes. And, although none of this was directed towards Pupi, the fact that he was sitting on the same sofa as her, made him feel fear by association and, with an elegant bow which no one else acknowledged, he made his way back behind the curtain he had come from, and disappeared from the scene altogether.

The Director continued, in a more agitated manner, "I have worked all of my life to create this earthly Eden and now you, you threaten to destroy it with your macabre faultiness, your insolent behavior, your shameful ways. Well, I am telling you, and you had better hear me loud and clear, there is absolutely no way I am going to let you do that!"

He stomped his fist against the coffee table again and Sybil jumped in her seat. All words had left along with Pupi's exit, perhaps also terrified of being seen in her presence, so she sat there in utter and petrified silence.

He continued, in strident tones, "You listen to me, and listen carefully: you will be getting a script tomorrow and you are going to memorize it like your life depends on it. We have to clean up the mess you made on your last two Streams and you are going to cooperate completely. If I detect so much as a fraction of you not following exactly what you are told to say, you will experience such horrific things that your mind has not even fathomed could be possible. Do you hear me?"

Sybil nodded as best she could as her palms perspired heavily, leaving a wet mark on her petalled dress.

The Director gave her one last menacing glance and said, "Now get the hell out of my sight." As he said so, he turned his back to her and looked out of his window once again.

Sybil gathered herself and, still shaking, made her way to the door, down the corridor and back to her chambers.

The Director pressed the intercom button.

The voice came through the static, "Yes sir."

"Wilhelm, double her medication. Schedule her Stream for two days from now. I will be there myself to make sure everything goes in order."

Chapter XVI

o o o

"Listen, Sybil. Listen to the sound of my voice. Anchor there. Listen."

I feel myself surrounded by warmth, my body slowly unfurling into the room that I am in.

"Very good, now tell me, what is your name?"

"Sybil."

"Sybil, get your Bridgepiece out for me. Ring it now."

The loud sound rings through my temples. I am momentarily drowsy, but his voice keeps me from fainting.

"Tell me, tell me what is your name?"

"My name is Blanchette."

"Very, very good. Okay Blanchette, describe to me what is happening around you."

"I am dressed in a beautiful red garment. My body is enveloped in the softest of fibers, from the tip of my toes to the very top of my

head, where a hood points its ruby-colored fabric up into the sky. I am warm, almost embryonic inside this exquisite red cloak.

"I am in my kitchen, watching my mother bake beautifully scented pastries and then place them, ever so delicately, in a basket. She smiles at me and hands me the baked goods and, with one last hug as I turn to face the door, she reminds me to never stray from the path."

"Very good, Blanchette. This is very important, remember that now. Ok, describe where you are now."

"I am walking through the cobblestone streets, watching my kind and happy neighbors wave at me as I go by. They all smile and send me good wishes as I walk along."

"Good, good. Tell me, why do they like you, Blanchette? Why do your neighbors smile at you and care for you so much?"

"Because I am Good and Innocent and I always follow the rules and have never done anything Wrong. They love how kind of a daughter I am, how well I behave, how generous and charming I am."

"Yes, yes you are. That is exactly what you are and always will be. A good and innocent girl. Now, tell me, where are you headed?"

"I am coming to the edge of the town. The cobblestone streets have finished and I am coming to the place where the wood begins. There is bramble everywhere. It is quite thorny as I walk through here and I spot small wild rose bushes as I go.

"Once you are through the bramble, what do you see?"

I am in a clearing. There is phosphorescent moss everywhere and lichen on all the tree barks.

Something in me relaxes completely. I look at the space around me and feel a lingering sensation of having been here before, of feeling at home in the wilderness around me. But I sense that I should not say this, so I keep quiet and simply look around.

"What are you doing now?"

"I am looking at some beautiful wild flowers, Lady's Slippers. I can't seem to stop looking at them, they are so exquisite to see."

"Blanchette, do you know what you are doing? Tell me what you have done."

I am flooded with panic, with a sense of terrible guilt. My stomach curls inside itself, my chest becomes tight.

"I...I...have strayed from the path."

"Yes, yes you have. Pay close attention, here, what did your mother say to you about this?"

"She told me never to stray from the path. I've been Bad, very Bad."

"Yes, this is absolutely Incorrect Behavior. Remember this, Blanchette. You should never do Bad things. What happens to little girls who do the wrong thing?"

"Terrible things happen to them."

"Yes they do. Yes they do…Now describe the scene you are seeing for me please, Blanchette."

"There is a shadow lurking under the shade of a tree. I can see two glowing eyes following my every move. The shadow moves towards the Sun and I see a…"

A part of me doesn't want to say the words. But I know I must. I know I must.

"I see a horrible, sinister, frightful wolf."

"And what do you know about him, Blanchette?"

Again, resistance.

"He is Evil."

"Indeed he is and we never want to associate with Evil. Tell me who he is."

"He is…he is the villain."

"Very good, Blanchette. He is the villain and we never, ever trust a villain. We ourselves want nothing to do with the villain or any of their evil actions. Now, where did he come from?"

"He came from the woods, from the deepest part of the wild. He is the villain who lives in the deepest, wildest part of the woods."

"That is correct, Blanchette. We know now that we never want to stray into the woods because that is where Evil lies. Remember this, you never want to go into the woods, dear, never. And what is this horrid creature saying to you?"

"He is asking about what I am doing. He is smiling in a sinister way and, when I tell him I am going to see my grandmother, he asks me where she lives. Once I tell him, he bids me farewell and saunters off back from where he came."

"And what do you do now?"

"I am continuing on my way. I am traversing the thick of the forest and come to the small path that leads to my dear Grandmama's house."

"I knock on the door and hear her voice from inside beckon me to come in. The house is completely dark, I can barely see. But I make my way in and search for my Grandmama in her kitchen, where she usually is. But she is not there and her voice comes again from her bedroom. She is asking me to come see her in bed, she is sick."

"I come closer to her, she is lying quite still in the bed. I ask her if there's anything I can do to help. She says to me that she would gladly accept my kindness and asks me to come into the bed with her.

"Her body is so stiff, she does not have the usual softness that I remember from her. And she has such strange eyes, such strange a smell, such strange teeth!"

"Yes, yes she does. When you see her strange teeth, what do you realize, Blanchette?"

"I realize that this is not my Grandmama I am laying next to, it is the terrible, villainous, treacherous wolf I saw before in the woods."

"Yes, and what do you realize now?"

"I realize I have made a grave mistake, that I should always follow the rules, that terrible things happen to those who break the rules, who do not listen to those that care for them, who stray off the path."

"Very, very good Blanchette. You are right, very right about what you have learned. And what happens now?"

"I need to learn my lesson. The wolf knows I have realized who he is and has opened his mouth wide. His yellow teeth are like tiny daggers that threaten to penetrate right through me and, in an instant, he has swallowed me whole. I slide down his innards and make my way all the way down into his fiery stomach, where I find my sweet Grandmama crying and huddled in the corner.

"I take her in my arms and we both cry about our great misfortune."

"What do you learn when you are there, holding your Grandmama in your great misfortune?"

"I see that, because of my misbehavior, not only am I suffering but I am making the people I love suffer too. I am making innocent people pay the price for my wrongdoing, when they are Innocent and Right and have done nothing to harm me."

"Good, very good. This is all very true. You must always remember this, Blanchette. Other people suffer if we do Wrong. You never want to do Wrong. You always want to do the Right thing. Always. And now, tell me, what do you hear?"

"There is a sound coming from the wolf's body. He is snoring. He is sound asleep and beginning to digest us. But there is another sound now too. It is the sound of the door opening, of someone calling out my Grandmama's name. It is the sound of a man coming into the cottage."

"Describe the sound of this man's voice to me."

"He is a hunter, here to save us. He is our hero. He is the man we have been waiting for. His voice is kind and benevolent. He sounds of pure compassion and care. I feel safe in the timbre of his presence. I hold my Grandmama and know that we will be saved."

"Very good. Yes he is. He is your hero. Heroes always know best and will always do what is Right. You can always trust the Hero. He is here to save you from the wild, savage wolf. Describe what is happening now, Blanchette."

"A beautiful light is pouring onto our bodies. A hole appears at the top of where we are trapped and the face of the kind and benevolent hunter looks down at us. He is holding an axe and opening the wolf's body.

"We emerge, completely unscathed. The hunter is smiling with so much kindness at us. He has pulled us out of the deep, wild, dark darkness that we were trapped in."

"And what do you know now?"

"Had it not been for him, we would be lost, unable to save ourselves."

"Correct. That is very correct. Very good! What is the hunter doing now?"

"He is asking me to get some rocks from outside and to bring them quickly."

I realize what is going to happen, what I am being asked to do, and again, I find resistance. But I know I must do what I am being asked. I know what I have to do.

"What are the rocks for, Blanchette? What do you have to do?"

"I have to kill the wolf. I have to kill him now."

"Very good. You do, you have to kill this wild wolf. What are you doing now?"

"I am filling the wolf's stomach with the heavy rocks and waiting for him to awaken. He does, eventually. And, when he does, he sees the hunter and immediately tries to run away. But he falls to the floor. The wolf is on the floor, pulled down by the heaviness of the rocks and he is slowly killed by them. From the inside out. He is killed from the center of the very place that we were just in."

"He is dying before you. And what do you know now?"

"I see that that dark, wild place within him was the very same place that killed him, that he died because he tried to bury us in the darkness."

"Yes, yes exactly. Now what is happening?"

"The hunter is taking the wolf's hide off. He is skinning him and is handing me the wolf's pelt. I am wearing it, I am wearing it like a hood."

"And now, we are reaching the end here Blanchette, what happens now?"

My Grandmama, the hunter and I walk back to our town. The hunter is holding me by the hand. The townspeople greet us with a shower of flowers. They are so grateful to the hunter for killing the terrible, bad wolf that had haunted them for so long. The hunter and I are getting married."

"Very, very good. And now what do you say, Blanchette?"

"And we lived happily ever after. The end."

"Wonderful. Now find your Bridgepiece again, Blanchette. Ring it for me now."

I ring the steel rod that I have had in my pocket all along and the sensation of nausea and throbbing pain in my head comes back.

"What is your name, dear?"

"Sybil."

"Sybil, good. Listen, Sybil. Listen to the sound of my voice. Anchor there. Listen. It is time to come back now. Come back, Sybil. Come back."

Chapter XVII

o o o

For three months Sybil's routine became inexorably repetitive. She grew accustomed to the beige lifestyle that had been rendered her new daily schedule. Gone were the exotic meals and exquisite gowns. Instead, a regulated diet became the norm. Her morning oatmeal was weighed on a scale and served to her in the same bowl, with the same spoon. Her meals became steamed vegetables and rice, and her dinner was the tiniest portion of carrot soup. All spices and flavors had been eliminated from her diet and, her biggest frill and choice, was the grand decision of whether or not to add salt to her meal, or not.

Her clothing had become regulated too. She was given four black jumpsuits which she could rotate over the week, and her hair was trimmed every two weeks to stay at the same length, always.

Exercise was a fixed routine too and, even her social experiences seemed to be regulated. It appeared as if the Beauticians had been explicitly told to be curt and only exchange the very basic modes of courteous speech with her and, when walking down the hall and meeting other Dreammakers, they all nodded politely and were quick to get on their way. Bella and Anne had particular hours that they would visit at and, Sybil thought, they seemed to be reciting a script that they had memorized for each of their encounters.

She could not quite put a finger on it, but she felt a dullness enshroud her whole mind. Although still clearly herself, as far as she could tell, something in her felt foreign, almost alien in her own skin, as if she were a mere tourist in the grounds that she used to inhabit. If she could have described it in words, she may have said that she felt like she had been caged into the cement holding room of lackluster, put on the leash of the habituated patterns of drab and trapped into the confines of utter and bleak homogeneity.

Chapter XVIII

o o o

It happened on the thirty-seventh time her Stream aired.

She arrived, as always, to the serious walls of the Office. Mr. Jacob had, as always, opened the door for her and showed her in with a curt head nod. Mr. Wilhelm was, as always, busily preparing his many machines that Sybil understood nothing about but that had appeared ever since her new Stream had aired. And finally, the Director sat in his cushioned chair, by the side of her reclining chair, proper and silent, as always.

On her first visit, she had tried to be amenable. She had smiled at the Director and tried to launch a conversation about the interesting weather patterns that she had been noticing in the past days and, as she watched her words fall flat on their faces, she picked them up gently from the floor and promised never to do that to them again. From then onwards, Sybil arrived in silence, was hooked up to the

Media Outlet in silence and, when she was done, would leave in silence.

Although feeling quite dull and incapable of processing much in the last months, there was a part of her that wondered and pondered what it was that she had done wrong. Try as she might, she could not come up with the reason for why things had changed so much for her and, although she had attempted to improve, it looked as if it had not been enough. And now this bizarre and incomprehensible routine had become her life.

She laid on the bed and waited for Mr. Wilhelm to hook her up to the many multicolored electrodes that always made Sybil feel like she was wearing some kind of bizarre polkadot helmet on her head.

Her eyes were affixed to the relentlessly white ceiling above her and, as she began to hear the familiar, dronish voice of the Director spill itself into her ear, counting down from ten to one, her eyelids became heavy and weighted, and, slowly, the cold Office space disappeared into the dark, warm place of her own mind.

¨Listen, Sybil. Listen to the sound of my voice. Anchor there. Listen.¨

I am embosomed by the luscious, saccharine smell of baking lavender. Beneath me are the well-masoned tiles of a floor that hold themselves in such a robust sense of human construction that, although made of earth, they feel deeply different from their source. I realize, in an instant, that this is my home.

"Very good, now tell me, what is your name?"

"Sybil."

"Sybil, get your Bridgepiece out for me. Ring it for me now."

I find the Bridgepiece, with its delicately cold fork shape and hit it against the wooden table next to me. The loud sound rings through my temples. I am momentarily drowsy, but his voice keeps me from fainting.

"Tell me, tell me what is your name?"

"My name is Blanchette."

"Very, very good. Okay Blanchette, describe to me what is happening around you."

"I am dressed in a beautiful red garment. My body is enveloped in the softest of fibers, from the tip of my toes to the very top of my head, where a hood points its ruby-colored fabric up into the sky. I am warm, almost embryonic inside this exquisite red cloak.

"I am in my kitchen, watching my mother bake beautifully scented pastries and then place them, ever so delicately, in a basket. She

smiles at me and hands me the baked goods and, with one last hug as I turn to face the door, she reminds me to never stray from the path.¨

¨Very good, Blanchette. Describe where you are now.¨

¨I am walking through the cobblestone streets, watching my kind and happy neighbors wave as I go by. They all smile at me and send me good wishes as I walk along.¨

¨Good, good. Tell me, why do they like you, Blanchette? Why do your neighbors smile at you and care for you so much?¨

¨Because I am Good and Innocent and I always follow the rules and have never done anything Wrong. They love how kind of a daughter I am, how well I behave, how generous and charming I am.¨

¨Yes, yes you are. Now, where are you headed?¨

¨I am coming to the edge of the town. The cobblestone streets have finished and I am coming to the place where the wood begins. There is bramble everywhere. It is quite thorny as I walk through here and I spot small wild rose bushes as I go.¨

My attention is caught by the wild rose bushes. They feel familiar, eerily familiar. A familiarity I have never experienced before, as if I knew them intimately, as if my skin and their skin had spent time in close communion, as if we had whispered tiny stories to each other and giggled under our breaths. I know those wild roses in ways that I cannot explain to myself and, although I know I must make my way and stay on the path, my whole body tarries at this spot that feels, in some way, like it is calling me, beckoning me in its soft-petalled tongue.

"Blanchette, once you are through the bramble, what do you see?"

I hear his voice. I know these words. I have heard them so many times before. I know what I have to do now, I have to move past the bramble, stay on the path, walk through the forest. I know this is what I must do, what I must say.

But my skin is being slowly caressed by this undomesticated vegetation and something inside me is pulsing with aliveness. I am listening intently to the croaking voice of the thorn, the crackling laughter of the branch, the soft lullaby of blossom. I do not want to leave.

"Blanchette, once you are through the bramble, what do you see?"

My eyes can make the path out perfectly. I see it in the simplicity of its trampled down existence - grass blade after grass blade trying to stand tall yet getting plodded over and over again by the weighted form of hunter moccasins, of young girl slippers.

I hear the urge in his voice, the line that demands another line, the question that is not a question but an order.

My feet are moving. I think I am moving toward the path, in the direction that I know I should go but, instead, I am making my way

deeper into the thicket of thorns and spines, deeper into the sinister
source of the wild rose bloom.

"Blanchette! Where are you going? Make your way
through the bramble now."

His voice pierces the sweet reverie I am in. As I make my way
deeper into the womb-like center of the thorn bush, his voice has gotten
stuck in the prickly edge of this spinous hedge and, although still loud,
like a giant balloon, it is slowly having the air taken out of it.

"Blanchette. You listen to me now, young lady. You
are going to turn around and walk right back here and then
you are going to do exactly as I tell you! Did you hear me?
Get back here now!"

I have lost sight of the path now, so thick are the branches and
the barks. His voice, although ferocious, seems to have lost all power to
sway me. I hear it, standing at the edge of where I am now, its throat
straining, its eyes bulging.

For a moment I wonder why this voice is so distant now, why
it is not here with me as it has always been in the past, right beside
every one of my actions, with me every place I go.

And as I stand there, embraced by the crisp shapes of rose
petals and honey locust trees, I realize that his voice will never reach me
here, it will never come close to where I am.

It is afraid.

"Blanchette! Blanchette!"

My body becomes, for the first time, a nest of softness. I feel an invisible clasp, like a hidden chain, break open and unravel before me, the weight of my bondage suddenly gone completely. A sense of emancipatory freedom penetrates my every pore and, the faintest of smiles, like a wild animal emerging from its hibernation, stretches itself across the canvas of my face.

"Blanchette! Sybil! You rogue miscreant! Get back here immediately! Sybil, you devil! You ungrateful fool! Get back here now!"

I listen to the waves of his voice crash against my bristly palace, feeling utterly protected by my organic walls. Slowly his voice becomes less audible, losing its robust constitution, becoming a gentle hum and then disintegrating altogether into utter silence.

I find myself crawling on all fours, going deeper and deeper into the vividly awake shadows that seem to invite me in, that seem to claim me in their vivacity.

As my body gets closer and closer to the earth beneath me, I am caught by a sudden urge to lay my body down on its solidity. Cheek so close to mud, forehead on ground, body resting on the bare naturalness of the moment. I slowly start to drift into a heavy, heavy sleep.

Chapter XIX

o o o

W ake up, Sybil. Wake up.¨

The voice is marshmallow syrup. It drips into my ear canal and fishes me out of the deep, motionless slumber I was in.

I breathe in the smell of musty earth, of burrowing mystery, of worm ecstasy. My feet, my hands, my spine feel different from anything I have ever known before. At the Company, I always felt ill at ease bathed in the perfumes and the body oils. And now, as I slowly regain consciousness, I feel my sinews creak and slither like orchid petals billowing in the playful wind and my feet, once heavy and grey, feel like the live wires of oak roots and vanilla pods.

I feel, strangely, well, alive.

¨Sybil, you there?¨

The voice is coming from somewhere behind the bramble. It is disembodied at the moment, for all my eyes can see is the thicket of thorny bush that separates me from it.

I try to speak, to answer, but my throat is dry and all I manage to croak out is a withered and hoarse monosyllable that could have been taken as a yes, I am here or no, I am disintegrating matter.

But the voice doesn't seem to mind my lack of linguistic ability and, instead, cheerily says, "Ah, good, you're awake. Been waiting for you for a while. You know you're a snorer? Would have taken me ages to find you had it not been for your rackety slumber sounds that led me right to you."

I feel embarrassed for a moment and recall Mr. Wilhelm's strict instructions to monitor myself and my behavior at all times, even when sleeping. "Ladies," he had once told me, "are dainty at all times, even in the deepest part of their repose."

The cheery tones of this voice, however, make me feel at ease, and the embarrassment is soon gone. I am slowly regaining the strength in my legs and I feel the curious urge to find the owner of the voice, to make my way out of my leafy nest.

I bring myself as close to the ground as possible and slowly start to crawl in the direction of the voice, getting mud and leaf debris splattered all over my face, hands and legs. As I make my way through the thicket, the thorns begin to pierce and grab at my red cloak, tearing it here and there, until soon the whole thing is threadbare, and completely fallen apart.

As I start to see the bush clear, a golden light peers here and there through the woven branches. My hand catches on a large thorn and the roundest, most radiantly carmine red drop of blood streams from the tip of my finger and lands, heavily, onto the earth beneath me.

I watch the drop coagulate in its strange, mythical, organic movements and mix itself with the terrene substance of soil. Something inside me knows that I am witnessing a dance that I do not fully understand, that whispers to me of a mystery, that draws me into the murmurs of something that I have heard only on the winged tips of a silent breeze, or on the dying rays of the Sun at dusk.

I am speechless and spellbound and also fully aware that something has happened that I do not know the words to, that is beyond the reach of what I understand.

It is the distinct sound of someone clearing their throat, very directly overhead of me, that draws me out of my reverie.

"You okay there, Syb?"

I look up, confused for a moment, having forgotten where I was and, through the meshed boughs and limbs, I see that someone is peering down at me. I catch a glimpse of a most unusual face and am immersed, for a moment, in the wave-like aroma of chrysanthemum perfume.

It is common to be able to define a face through its features, to pinpoint the references that make up someone's unique visage, to create a map, using the landmarks of their forehead, cheekbones and jaw. And, expecting to use this methodology again, I go about tracing the features before me, only to find a baffling mixture of seeming contradictions all smiling calmly down at me.

The face above me has the softest of foreheads, as if made of rabbit fur or ivory fluff. However, it is also deeply creased, as if made from the edges of crags, or the depths of jagged rock. The nose is exquisite and fine, chiseled and delightful. However, it is also rough and the nostrils appear to be uncommonly large. The mouth is a delicate azalea petal, whose lips are cracked and parched. The cheekbones are made out of oyster dust, but snaggy and jutted as they stand high above it all. And the eyes, perhaps the most incomprehensible feature of them all, are both infinitely deep, fished out of the octopus' underwater lullaby, and also light, seductive, as if plucked out of a flirtatious daisy field and mixed in the strange booze of absinthe and rum.

Needless to say, I cannot, for the life of me, figure out who, or even what, it is that is looking down through the bush. However, their presence is benign and, the part of me that was always on alert when I was at the Company, the part of me that always felt like it had to be on its best behavior, to act in perfect form, to be on guard, is soothed and softened in their presence.

"You gonna stay there all day?" The voice, who now has a face, asks.

Another smile beams down at me and, unable to say why exactly, I take it as an invitation to make my way through the last stretch of the bramble. As I do so, the last bits of fabric that make up my clothing also get pulled off by the relentless thorns and I emerge from the thicket, naked, covered in nothing but mud and bits of dried leaves.

Again, a wave of embarrassment floods through me, but it is the steady gaze of the being before me that puts me at ease and, suddenly, I feel like I am perfectly dressed for the occasion.

I am met by another smile, perhaps warmer than any of the ones before and, with a nod, I hear the words, "Yes, indeed, you are perfectly dressed for the occasion."

It is then that I decide to stand up and behold the voice's owner fully. Just as the face had been a mystery of features, the body that I have before me is no different.

They are dressed in a golden mantle made of, what seem to be, yellow fish scales. The attire reminds me of something I have seen before but I cannot quite recall where. Their hands are mighty, strong and firm, yet delicate and tender at the same time. The feet are bare and visibly calloused on the bottom, yet finely polished and impossibly soft. And as my eyes follow the torso, I am flooded by the distant sensation of familiarity, as if this body were not as foreign to me as I deemed it to be. My eyes follow the landscape of chest and ribs and I see, clearly, the form of firm breasts protruding out of the fine, golden garment and, in an instant, I know I have seen this shape before.

A melodious laugh emerges from the sweet mouth with cracked lips.

"Yes, yes. You most definitely have seen me before, Sybil. Many times, actually. You don't remember most of them, but I did manage to crack through that thick mind of yours from time to time. Not your fault, really. Anyone with the level of medication that you were under would have been as bogged down and out of it as you were. But hey, you prevailed! And look at you now! Butt naked in the middle of the forest, standing in front of a person that you can't quite make out if they are a man or a woman, dehydrated, extremely confused, separated from everything you have known in your life. Hurrah, Syb. Well done!"

Chapter XX

o o o

W ell, I guess we should get to the bit that everyone always seems to get hung up on at the beginning." I receive another smile, a hint of a wink, and all I can do is stand there, quasi mesmerized, watching the enchanting mouth open and close as it formulates words. "Having suckled on the breast of duality for so long, it is hard to put me in a comfortable, digestible category for you. Used to the 'This or That', the 'A or B', or convinced that you only get to choose between vanilla or chocolate ice cream, well, I show up, blow your mind, and tell you that I simply don't fit into any of those, apparent, options.

"Within such a limited view, I ask you, what of the rest of the alphabet? What of the legions of flavors that live in the ice cream shop's cellar?

"I am the XYandZ, and also the PQRS. I am the cookie dough and papaya slushie, the mandarin gelato with a cashew twist served over a medium spice waffle sundae. I am the bubble gum and maracuya sherbert combo you never imagined was possible.

"Am I a woman? No. Am I a man? No. Am I both? Nope. Am I neither? Nah. I'll tell it to you as it is, Syb, plain and simple: I am what I am."

It may have been the way the light was hitting my eyes, but I am pretty sure the golden-robed being in front of me just took a curtsy.

Knowing not what to do, I find myself holding out my hand and stammering the words, "Ni...ni...nice to meet you."

A big bubble of a chuckle emerges from the pleasant mouth and a hand comes out to meet mine. It is both deliciously delicate and firmly calloused. It shakes my own hand, actually, my entire arm, vigorously and heartily, seemingly quite delighted to partake in this ritual.

"Nice to meet you too, Sybil!" Another rolling laugh leaps out of the robed being's throat and scurries off on the forest floor.

"How...how do you know my name?" My arm is back by my side and I am suddenly aware that this being has been calling me by my name the whole time and, it is not until now, that this seems utterly surprising.

"Oh Sybil, Sybil. I know so much more than just your name. In fact, I know so much about you it could be argued that we are quite well acquainted already. I know it does not seem that way to you now, but you'll come to get my meaning soon enough."

This enigmatic answer does nothing for me except plunge me into more confusion and, swimming in the waves of uncertainty, I reach out for something that will make me feel like I have a grip on anything, even the smallest of things.

"Well, since you know my name, would you care to share yours with me?" I say, hoping that will give me a place to land.

Yet another big smile in the already long parade of grins. This one is long and horizontal, and highlights the high arches of the delicate cheek bone structure.

"What is it with all of you and your obsession with naming things? It's like, here we are, in a place and moment in time that neither of us have ever experienced before, floating along in the great, well-seasoned soup of the unknown, perhaps closer to the mystery than you have ever been before and yet, there you go, not even five minutes into the whole thing, and you start pointing that little index finger of yours, wanting to know thing's names or, if you don't know their genus, their kingdom, their species, making up names yourself. As if all that could save you from the big, uncomfortable feeling of drowning in the great I Don't Know is your indexical power that suddenly makes everything safe and understandable again. Mere pretense, really. That shore that you want to swim onto is pure quicksand, babe. Don't throw your anchor there, it ain't as solid as you think.

"There was this one guy here who arrived a long time ago, went by the name of Adam back then. When he first arrived, oh man, all he'd do, all day long, was run around, pointing at things and naming them as if there were no tomorrow. Good grief, you'd think the guy would get over it after a while, but I guess when all you've heard your whole life is that you need to make sense of everything around you, the habit's hard to kick.

"When he did finally start to kick the old addiction, boy oh boy, his brain turned into utter goo. So exhilarating to watch. Man was turned into a big, bumbling baby, drooling over everything, wide eyed, mesmerized, finally quiet after ages of endless taxonomical dribble. It was beautiful, I tell you. Absolutely beautiful. An incredibly sacred thing to witness…"

A long moment of silence drops between us and, unsure of what to do, I fidget, and a tiny twig cracks under my foot.

The sound snaps the robed being back, head shakes, eyes focus back on me and then the words, "Oh, got lost there in that sweet memory for a second. Anyway, yes, you were asking me something. Right, my name, what is my name. OK, well, I guess I can play that game. But let's not take it too seriously. You with me?" A wink comes straight at me and I nod, finding myself smiling a small but real smile.

"Well, some people around these parts call me Tiriesias, and quite a few call me Ti. Then there is a whole crowd of people that don't really ever call me anything. So, whatever you prefer really, it makes absolutely no difference to me."

Since I have been given the choice, I take another look into the big, mystery-laden eyes and decide to go for, "Ti".

"Look," says Ti, "since we're on the whole matter of man and woman and the he and she thing, I think I oughta let you know that I wasn't a big fan of you running around telling your friends that you had 'seen Him', every time I appeared. Especially not with a big capital H, as if I were some kind of big ol' archetypal superstar or whatnot."

A flashback of me sitting in bed, sweating in Bella's arms suddenly swoops in, out of nowhere, and prances around in my memory.

¨I mean, I get it. Every time I made an appearance in the delicate seams of your mind, the only place you could put me was in the 'he' category. We are, indeed, products of our conditioning, until, of course, we choose not to be. And, I get it, you had been groomed into believing yourself to be a princess. It makes sense you'd think that a 'him' was always about to appear, about to swoop you off your feet, take you into la la land, save you from your current circumstance, yada yada yada. But, just to be clear: That's not who I am. Not in the least. I am not a 'him', for starters, and I am not here to save you from anything because there ain't nothing to save you from in the first place, Syb. I know this is probably not making much sense to you right now but, what I just said is kinda the whole point of you being here in the first place, ok? Let's just get this clear: I'm not going to swoop you off your feet, I'm not here to save you, and I am not here to welcome you into la la land. None of that, got it?¨

I am looking at Ti with unblinking eyes and realize that, just as they pointed out, most of what was just said to me has gone completely over my head. Yes, I understand the words themselves, but the real meaning of what was just said seems to dance right out of my reach and I am suddenly overwhelmed by the inexorable realization that I have never been in this place inside myself before. I am in a territory where I have never treaded but that I knew always existed. I see, for the first time in all the while I have been here, standing naked next to a hedge of bramble, that I am at the farthest edge of where I have ever explored within my own bounds and I am both utterly terrified and completely exhilarated, all at the same time.

Chapter XXI

∘ ∘ ∘

The Sun is coming down on us directly from above, as if the sky is pouring down luminous carrot juice through the forest canopy. We have been in ecstatic silence now for quite a while and midmorning is knocking at the door. Ti takes it as a queue to speak again.

¨Well Syb, I have to say, for a newbie, I am quite surprised at how quickly you ran out of questions there. Usually it's a floodgate of how's and why's and where's and with whom's, but being in silence here with you for all this time has been quite, well, refreshing. Nice.¨

I am pretty sure that I just got another wink from those big leopard eyes.

I take my first, real look around at my surroundings after all this time and realize that I am not in the kind of woods that I had seen before in my Streams. There is something distinctly different about the vegetation and soil here, almost as if this woodland were breathing, pulsing, speaking through its verdant nature.

"Yes, very true," says Ti, as if answering my thoughts, "It is very much the woodland living that you are perceiving. Could never have noticed that before, in the state you were in but now, well, now you can see it with your very own eyes. Majestic, isn't it?"

I nod vehemently and take a step toward one of the giant oak trees closest to me, but Ti quickly stops me in my tracks.

"Now, now, let's not get too ahead of ourselves. I have no intention of stopping your wish to get closer to that tree, please don't misunderstand me. It's just that, well, we are kinda at the Edge here and I'm not sure if you've realized that yet."

I give Ti a quizzical look and ask, "The Edge?"

"Yeah, you know, it's kinda like a crossroads, this spot we're at. One of those symbolic things. I mean look at it, it's pretty obvious: on the one side you have the path you came on, the road, the town and, also the Company, the people you've known, the kind of food you've grown accustomed to. Then there is this bizarre fence-like thing made up of bramble and thorns and whatnot, right at the edge of the woods, that in between spot, that place where the town ends and the woods begin. And then, right where you were about to go and get closer to that oak tree, there starts a whole different world, full of shadows, and creatures and things you have no clue about yet. See it now?"

I do see it now. I realize I am at the fulcrum spot, the place where, whatever step I take in one direction is a decision to leave the in between place and walk well, Somewhere.

"Now, let me be really clear here now, Syb. In case you're about to fall into the same folly of that whole chocolate and vanilla conundrum we mentioned before. It may seem like there is a 'This path' or 'That path' kinda thing going on. And, maybe you're even starting to fall into an old mental habit and start to think that there is a 'Better path' or a 'Worse path' to take. Let me just get all of that mumbo jumbo out of your mind right now and tell you that there is none of that stuff going on here. You are free to walk straight into the woods, you are free to walk right back into the Director's arms, you are free to dance a polka, shoot the breeze, and hang out here for the rest of eternity. Heck, you can even curl yourself up into a little ball and sleep in that little nest of yours for the rest of your life and, guess what, that's also perfectly fine."

Maybe it's the fact that I have not blinked for a while, or that I have just stood here staring at Ti without speaking, or the fact that I have Mr. Wilhelm's face appearing in my memory telling me just the opposite of what I just heard, "There is always a Right choice and a Wrong choice, Sybil. And you are here to make the Right choice, to make us all proud, to be Good and to set the example for everyone watching your Stream..." Maybe it was all of that combined that made Ti feel the need to go on and clarify even more.

"Okay look, I'm clearly going to have to convince you on the matter and give you some more supporting evidence for you to even begin to grasp what it is that I just said. Show me what you have in your hand."

A wave of absolute panic takes over me. I am sweating and wide eyed. How could Ti possibly know that I have something in my hand? The only person ever to know that I had something in my hand was my Teller and I was specifically instructed never, ever to...

"Yes, yes, never ever to show what you have in your hand to anyone, especially not someone in your Stream." Ti says, "And well, I guess we technically still are in some version of your Stream and yes, technically, you have been told that showing what you have in your hand to anyone would compromise your mind to edges where no Teller could ever help you and all that stuff. But have you ever wondered, Syb? Have you ever glided your fingertip on the cold, metal object you have in your hand and wondered what would happen if you ignored what you had been told?

¨I know you did. You also felt it when you would look at the ambiguous faces morphing around into unfocusable goop in your Stream. I know a part of you wanted to break that rule too. ´Never, ever look at someone in your Stream in the eye. Never focus your attention or you will wreak havoc on your mind.’ Etcetera, etcetera. But the temptation was almost irresistible. Am I right?¨

Memories of endless Streams where I could feel a part of me resisting all of my training, all of my instructions, come drifting, like a dainty parade of nimbus clouds, through my thoughts. And it is as if, for a moment, that is all I can feel. I am covered, from head to toe, in the memory of my resistance, of my wish to break the rules. I look at Ti again, as if searching for an answer to a question I can’t quite phrase.

¨Perhaps it would make more sense if I explained why those rules are there in the first place, instead of keeping you here, in the hidden confusion of you simply being told that you had to follow them.¨ Ti cleared their throat and stands up a little taller, a little more regally. ¨Those rules are there to prevent things like that little escapade of yours that you pulled some hours ago from ever happening. I mean, for all intents and purposes, you've basically just exited your script, Syb."

With everything that had been happening during this morning, I had not even stopped to think about that. Now, it is all plundering down on me in one big, fell swoop.

Ti continues, "Most interestingly of all, and this Syb, I gotta hand it to you, was most impressive and truly hilarious, was that you did it live on prime time over National Streaming Service!"

Ti's lips part and the loudest, most exuberant laugh emerges from somewhere deep inside that unique body of theirs and has, just as their body, a multiplicity of seemingly opposing tones happening all at the same time. Their strident laugh is the strange marriage of a cockatoo trying to bark out a Shakespearian sonnet while a host of tiny footed flamenco dancers try to tap out a morse code message to a far off lover. It is both a cacophony and a perfect symphony all rolled up into one and, when it stops, the emptiness it leaves behind is almost eerie.

Ti takes a deep breath in, adjusts the robe that has gone slightly awry in all the commotion, and then goes on as if nothing happened, "Those rules are there to keep every Dreammaker on task. It is much easier to lead someone along if they are semi dazed and mostly confused, unable to focus on anything and terrified of ever doing anything wrong. So, naturally, those rules are there to make that job much easier.

"Look at it this way, Syb, if you'd been able to focus your attention on those faces that would appear in your Stream, if you'd been able to, just for one second, realize that you had the power to control your mind within one of your Streams well...Would you have been so easily persuaded to follow what your Teller was saying to you ever again? Would you have willingly given up your whole sense of personal freedom within your Stream to someone who's not even there, who is just a disembodied voice ordering you around all over the place? Nope? Thought so. Of course not! Easy math there: keep the Dreammaker as unaware of their capacity to know what they can truly do with their own mind and the world around them and there you have it, infinite serfdom forever."

I realize I am being told something of earth shattering proportions, but all I can do at the moment is swallow hard and blink slowly from time to time. Ti realizes that I am not quite suited to keep the conversation rolling and so, continues on.

"Ok, so now that that's clear, it might be easier for you to understand more about that thing that you have in your hand, your Bridgepiece."

In all of my time at the Company, there was a subject that was never discussed with anyone, not with our Beauticians, not with our fellow Dreammakers, not even with our Tellers once we were out of our Stream. There were clear instructions, "You never talk about your Bridgepiece."

"Remember that time," Ti says, interrupting my reverie, "when you were instructed to play your Bridgepiece and it was as if you'd just been told to swallow lead?"

The memory is all too vivid. And, oddly, it is not just one memory, but hundreds of them that flood me all at once.

"Well, Syb, I know you're not in the least bit used to this and this might boggle your brains up for a while but hey, we have all the time in the world, so boggle away. I'm gonna let you in on a little secret: Not once in your entire career as a Dreammaker did you ever want to play that Bridgepiece of yours but, you did it. You did it every single time to please your Tellers, to get those nice, comforting words said to you, to be told that you were Good and that you were doing the Right thing. And, every single time, you just swallowed that big gulp of lead straight down into that little, gullible body of yours and went on with the show, pretending like nothing was happening. Well I'm here to tell you Syb: plenty was happening."

I feel woozy. More than woozy. Hours of my training are flushing around inside me like a stormy sea, whisking me around in their delirium. I am seeing the smiling faces of Mr. Wilhelm and Mr. Jacob. I am remembering the first time we ever met and how they told me they were there to take care of me, to protect me from everything that could ever harm me. I am vividly remembering my first warm meal and the words of reassurance that I would always be safe, that all I had to do was follow instructions and I never had to worry about anything ever again. I am remembering the silent tears in my room, the tears I never told anyone about because it was Wrong to be sad or confused. I remember the disparate feelings of a great weight being taken off of me, of finally feeling warm and safe after years of hunger, cold and exile, but the great price I was asked to pay to feel that. And the strange memories that I could never understand: the strange and inexplicable part of me that missed my black, plastic bag, and my, my....

"...own thoughts and wild dreams, is what you're thinking there, Syb." Ti finishes my sentence. "I know those are pretty frontier thoughts you are having there. You're basically at the edge of what you can think of right now, after so much training and tuning. I know it's a place you've been told never to visit so it is hard for you now to even formulate those words. I know it's tough at the beginning.

But, believe me, it gets easier as you become more familiar with yourself again. Soon, you'll be finishing your own sentences." The kindest grin pops out of Ti's face and caresses my cheeks and forehead. I feel like I have never been smiled at like this before. I feel like the smile is, actually, genuine.

A ringing courage takes over me after receiving that smile and I say, "Will you tell me about the Bridgepiece, Ti? I'd like to know."

Ti looks at me with a twinkle in their eye and says, "Sure, Syb, sure I can."

Chapter XXII

o o o

Limmm....llliiiiiii....liminnnn....lllllliiiiim....liminal."

Ti's mouth is moving in all sorts of shapes and forms. One moment the tongue is high on the palette, the next the lips are softly pursed together and humming, and the next, the cheeks are pulled far apart and a loud, emerging vowel fills up the space between the uvula and the teeth.

"Try it, Syb. It's one of my favorite words. To be honest, I kinda have a crush on it, it's so damned sexy. All of those close-mouthed consonants and those coquettish vowels stitched together in one very delightful word. Not to mention what it means. Good old denotation yum yums, this word is. Gets me a bit turned on, to be honest. Limmm....limminallll....liminal."

I guess I'll give it a go and find my own mouth performing wild gymnastics and, after a while, I can see why Ti likes this word so much.

¨You know what it means?¨ Ti shoots me a penetrating glance.

I shake my head and my well-measured bob goes swoosh, swoosh.

¨The word 'liminal' comes from the Latin word *limen*, meaning threshold. It's any point or place of entering or beginning. A liminal space is the time between the 'what was' and the 'what will be.' It is a place of transition, a season of waiting and not knowing.¨

Ti is looking up into space, intoxicated from that definition and, since I am not sure what any of this has to do with the Bridgepiece, I clear my throat and Ti comes back, slightly startled, from their reverie.

¨Oh my, sorry about that. Sorry, Syb. I've got this kind of courtship thing going on with language. And, honestly, any time I get to flirt around a bit with a word that is quite to my liking, well, it really takes over all that I am doing. My apologies though, I know you're waiting for me to get on with my point.

¨Well, anyway, moving along. Liminal. Yes, well, this word is quite related to both the Bridgepiece and this moment now. Look at what's going on here with me, won't you, Syb? I mean, here we are, two people, standing at the edge of the forest. You just took off and left, mid-Stream, and crawled through a, dare I say it, quite a huge amount of thorny bush there, for no real rhyme or reason. Now you're getting your whole sense of the familiar getting knocked around inside you so you don't know what the heck to really believe in anymore. You've been given the choice between going or staying here, there or anywhere and, also, I don't know about you, but my guts are rumbling, I'm feeling hungry and I have no idea if I'll be getting any food any time soon. Liminal. See? We're standing smack down in the middle of the huge I Don't Know."

I take in what Ti is pointing out and say, "I guess so, yes. And, how does this all relate to the Bridgepiece?"

"Oh right, you're getting impatient with me there. Yes, I know, I know. I'm a bit of a rambler. It's a habit I picked up once I realized there was never a point to get to and that I had all the time in the world to never get there. But I know it bugs people sometimes so I'll try my best to stick to a topic and keep digressions to a minimum." Ti's eyebrows do a quirky dance on the porcelain forehead they call home and then Ti goes on, "Ok, so, the Bridgepiece. Well, the whole idea of the Bridgepiece came around after Walt, sorry, the Director, as you know him, had been 'working' on people for a while. See, once you start messing around with folks' minds for some time you come to realize that there is a part of it that is clean cut, presentable and manageable, and then there is a whole other part in there that is well, a downright mess of a freaking shit show in there.

"The Director came to realize that that place was just a bit too much to deal with. I get it, don't blame him in the least. I probably would have come to the same conclusion myself had I not had the very bizarre personality that I have. But, that's beside the point. To make a long story short, and I'm pretty sure the Director has filled you in on quite a bit of his own story so it's not like I am spoiling any of this for you by telling you some of the behind the scenes here, after some years of building up the Company, the Director came up with the idea of the Bridgepiece.

"To implement the idea, he basically had to cordon off whole areas of the mind that were well, just not quite able to be worked with or made any prettier. That was the whole point, you know. The Director was there to help people work with themselves, help improve them, help make them better. Sweet intention. Good guy. But when he'd managed to work with the, let's say, more superficial layers of people's problems, then the real muck and grime came to the party and the Director's own hopes and dreams, his own finish line, got pulled out from under him. I guess you could say that the Director had the idea to make people 'perfect,' 'problem-less,' if you will. When, after years of work, more stuff, the deeper, more grotesque and macabre stuff, started to show up, he decided to take a short cut and hence, the Bridgepiece."

Ti's hand is pointing at my own hand and, although resisting the urge and wrestling inside myself, I suddenly feel compelled to open my fist and show Ti and the woods around me my own, personal, Bridgepiece.

It is shining in the Sun's rays beautifully. It is, as always, gleaming and perfectly solid. Made up of two prongs and one little handle. Its metallic surface rings out in its own quiet potential.

"You would not know this, because this was many years before your time," says Ti, "but this used to be called a 'tuning fork'. That was back when people used to play things called, 'instruments' and make music with their own bodies and voices. Magical things would happen when people would choose to partake of such an activity. The sheer memory of it sends chills down my spine. It's like nothing you have heard before, Syb. People expressing themselves, using their lives to make something of absolute beauty for no other reason than the edification of that moment in time. See, all of that disappeared because it was deemed, well, pointless.

"The concepts though, remained. The Director was masterful in taking over many of the domains of the arts, and music was, perhaps, his biggest acquisition."

For a moment, it seems like Ti is about to take the Bridgepiece into their hands but then stops.

"Let me tell you a little about how this tuning fork used to work," Ti says. "Before the Bridgepiece was what it is today, this little piece of metal was used to tune instruments. One would strike it against a surface, put it against one's ear and the tuning fork would always ring out in a specific frequency. The point is, this was always a reliable pitch and, no matter where your instrument had dallied off in its tuning, you could always hear this tone, readjust your instrument to it and then be completely assured that you were in the same frequency. Every instrument could do it and then you would know that you were all playing on the same, reliable ground, you could say. From that solid, common ground, more notes could be added that would create harmonies, and melodies and then a great majestic language of expression could arise from there with limitless possibilities. As I said, it was breathtaking.

"Well, the Director used some of these principles and applied them to humans, and that's when the tuning fork started to be called the Bridgepiece. Remember what I was telling you about that whole underground psychic shit show that I mentioned before?¨

I nod and Ti goes on, ¨Well, the Director discovered a way to put all that away in a psychic cabinet file, if you will. All the weird psychic anomalies, the strange fixations, the exotic fetishes, the bizarre psychoses, were all corralled up and put under lock and key. The thing about this is that it turned into a very easy way for the Director to put away, basically, anything he didn't want to deal with. Soon mild manias, obtuse obsessions, trivial ticks and innocuous imbecility were also put away in there and, then, all the Director had to deal with was pretty mild-mannered, superficial, psychological stuff that is so easy to work with and so manageable and so very much what he had always dreamed of. He had created perfect people who were always decent, always well-behaved, incredibly productive, and absolutely happy to be part of the status quo. It was heaven for him.¨

Ti pauses. The woods take a breath. A small sparrow takes flight.

¨I think I'm missing the part where the Bridgepiece comes in, Ti,¨ I say.

¨Yes, of course, that's because they haven't arrived on the scene just yet. For a while there, everything was running smoothly. The Director was pleased as punch, people were all high functioning and the picture of perfection. That is, until things started to fall apart at the seams. See, what the Director hadn't counted on was the fact that, the more stuff he'd corralled away from people's direct access, the more it would just fester away in the fetid labyrinth of repression. Bizarre anomalies would start to crop up in the most unexpected of places: a top executive would suddenly turn rabid and rip his shirt off while trying to count backwards from one thousand thirty-one; a perfectly well-mannered secretary would try to dye her hair with red pen ink and obsessively attempt to stick her toes in her mouth; a model Consumer would throw themselves into the middle of the street to wrestle his own shadow while at the same time trying to make out with it. You get the picture.

"Needless to say, the situation was a bit sticky and the Director was not happy with what he was seeing. An important lesson was learned because of these freakish outbursts though: the Director could not put the stuff he didn't want to deal with under lock and key and then walk away and pretend like it wasn't going to fester like an old forgotten Evening Delight packet left in the back of the Cooler.

"No, he had to come up with another plan, and so, the Bridgepiece appeared and, with it, the Dreammaker format that you are now familiar with. Hey, you thirsty?"

Ti is pulling out a picnic basket from under their robes and taking out two large flasks, filled to the brim with water. I am handed one and drink it to the very last drop. I had not realized how thirsty I was.

"Told you my belly was rumbling," Ti says. "Come on, let's have a picnic, a liminal picnic if you will, while I tell you the rest of the story."

We are sitting down now, Ti in the fish-scale robe, me stark naked and the oddest assortment of edibles streaming out of the cornucopia basket that both entice me and completely confuse me. Ti is pulling out a fried oyster mushroom with string bean and almond yoghurt parfait. Next to it sits a nasturtium and wild spinach pudding. A tapioca casserole is being handed to me that smells of cookie dough and soy sauce. Ti encourages me to take a spoonful of it but I decide to pass.

"So, as I was saying," Ti is now eyeing the picnic contents laid out in front of us and is choosing a plate of cranberry and tofu tapas, "That's when the Dreammakers came in. Very smart man, the Director. He brought the subjects into the Company and gave them exquisitely pampered and profoundly regimented lives. And he allowed these women to dip into their psychic lagoons under what you now know as Extractions. From there, the Director would actually be able to watch everything that was going on in there, then medicate the subjects into absolute oblivion so that they could not remember a single thing they had seen there and then, wham, the Streams were created.

¨This is, finally, where the Bridgepiece comes in, Syb. Hand me one of those asparagus crackers, won't you?¨ As Ti munches, I take another look at the Bridgepiece that glistens in my hand. ¨The Streams were a brilliant move. I am sure the Director has boasted about them to you. Basically, it was a very controlled way to be able to dip into the dark shadows of the mind without it wreaking havoc on the very, very controlled minds of any Consumer. Just as the Director had done with the more superficial aspects of the mind, he discovered he could lead anyone through these obscure places and still make sure that all ethical and moral values were still in place and, not only that, but actually seeping into this obscure territory. Hence, the script: basically a rewritten and completely manicured tour of our fears, our desires, our repressed hopes, our skewed beliefs.

¨What's the best way to face something you are afraid of? You subdue it into total predictability. You dissect it with logical patterns, you basically make it innocuous by completely domesticating it.

¨The thing was, when the Director tried to lead anyone with a script, it would always backfire on him. The

Dreammaker would always rebel and do whatever she wanted. So, a link needed to be made between the dark places of the mind and the Stream that was being performed. The Bridgepiece served to, literally, bridge these two worlds together.

"Remember at what point in your script you play your Bridgepiece?" Ti asks.

"Right after I am asked my name." I answer.

"Indeed, in that moment, you are still fully aware of being you and that you are in a Stream and, basically, you could do anything you'd like right there and then. You'd be lucid. Very dangerous stuff! But the Director added this sound, the ringing of the tuning fork to, as he says, tune you. To what? Not to A440, I'll tell you that much. No. It's a bit weirder than that actually. He actually tuned the tuning forks to the sound that the mind makes right at the moment in between a dream and waking: the liminal state."

Ti pops a puffed jalapeño macaroon into their mouth and munches happily for a minute or two.

"This is where it gets downright macabre, Syb. See, what the Director realized was that, as soon as that sound rang through, anyone was susceptible to being led anywhere he pleased. And, not only that, but he had full access to the very superficial part of the mind as well as to that very deep part of the mind. Man is a genius. He even changed Dreammaker's names so that they'd feel completely dissociated from themselves, unable to even have the slightest grip on who they are. That Director, I tell you, he really knows his stuff."

A tempura blueberry gets whisked up and dropped into Ti's mouth and they continue, "In this way, he could inoculate anyone, at any level, with whatever he wanted. His dream was to have a perfect society so that's what he created: beautiful maidens who are incapable of making any decision for themselves, princes who are virile and powerful, mothers who are perfect at baking and at showing unconditional compassion, fathers who are the heads of the household and are always right. He created his living, breathing heaven on earth."

I am slowly munching on a pumpkin cracker and try to make sense of everything that was just said to me. The words that I have just heard sit heavily inside me, their weightiness making it almost impossible for me to eat, I feel so full.

I notice my eyes are getting heavy and, as I turn to look at Ti, I receive the most incomprehensible of smiles, a wave of their dove-like hand, and their coquettish voice saying, "Bye bye."

A moment later, I am fast asleep under the canopy of oak and ash trees as the dusk starts to play hide and seek among the trunks of the trees and the light green hues of the dancing leaves.

Chapter XXIII

o o o

Bramble. I am in a thicket of wild rose bushes and honey locust bark. I can feel the harsh web of thorns around me as they pierce my flesh if I move too fast or too abruptly. I learn quickly and make my body silky, soft, allowing the net of thistles to slowly disentangle itself from my fur.

I hear him first. His heavy leather boots make a dissonant chord in the symphonic orchestration of opossum hymn, owl melody and cricket choir. He is corpulent and strangely agile in his cumbrous body, creating an arrhythmic pulse in the beat of the woodland at night.

Then I smell him. I am surprised at my own mouth salivating voraciously, as if commanded by some unknown appetence that draws me to him and also keeps me safely distant. He smells of the tangy substance of old blood, the perfume of carcass, the essence of death. On his shoulder lies the body of a young deer, eyes empty, guts slowly dripping thick, fresh juices onto his soiled shirt.

I follow him to his hut and watch him from the voyeuristic distance of his thick glass windows as he slowly, artfully, cuts through the meat, the bones and viscera, making untidy piles all around him.

I discover an ache inside my own meat, bones and viscera and surprise myself wishing he would look out the window, see me with his huntsman eyes, catch me, wrestle me, prey upon me as I prey upon him.

The desire becomes so vividly wild, so full of vitality, that my mouth purses its lips and I send out a long and feral howl.

Chapter XXIV

o o o

I bolt up and am shocked back into the morning sun peering at me from the high places of the trees above. The gentle rays in their syrupy splendor are drizzling onto me, bathing me in the sweet decadence of warmth and glow.

"Morning, Syb. You look like a proper stack of pancakes there, hun. Actually, come to think of it, I have just the thing for the occasion." Ti's voice is like cinnamon this morning. A moment later, I am hit with the heavy aroma of fresh baked goods tickling my insides with their chubby scents as Ti holds out a platter of waffles, scones and muffins for me to eat.

I am hesitating, hungry but also unable to resist the question that is aching to pop out into the morning air.

"Did you…did you hear me, Ti? Did I…did I just… did I just howl?" The question rolls around on the floor, performing some acrobatic swivels, a couple of pirouettes and then landing in a perfect split in the space between Ti's calm face and my own concerned countenance.

Ti looks down at the question, picks it up and places it in one of the many pockets of their golden dress. It seems nothing I say is not met with a smile, and this one, crisp in the morning breeze, as if freshly baked alongside the rest of the pastries sitting beside us, has the strange effect of comforting and confusing me all at the same time.

"Oh I heard you, Syb. Probably everyone and every thing in the whole darned forest heard you." Ti pauses for a second as a twinkle, a glimmer, a mischievous gleam struts through their eyes, and then, in something close to a raucous whisper, they say, "It was marvelous!"

A wave of relief passes through me and, as it's done with the tour of my insides, something else comes to the fore. It is so foreign, so obtuse in its nature, so completely incomprehensible to me that there is nothing I can do to keep it inside. I cannot keep it chained or restrained anymore. Without warning, I find a laugh erupting forth from me, jiggling and wobbling on my lips and tongue and then cascading onto the moss below.

The feeling is so extraordinarily unusual that I am shocked at the way my body shakes and wheezes, bouncing up and down in a fantastic cadence. To my astonishment, Ti joins me too and soon we are on the floor, our hands on our stomachs, loud chuckles, strident snickers and loud whooping all making their way through the shrubbery and the dense underbrush around us.

"Oh my. Oh my goodness, Syb. You really are a piece of work. That's truly fantastic."

At this point, my laughter has calmed down enough for me to remember my original question and I am back to being confused.

"Ti, what in the hell was that? I mean, it appears to be so strange but also oddly familiar and not weird at all. What the hell is going on?"

Ti has settled down onto a nice big swatch of old lichen and is looking at me directly, gauging me and taking their sweet time to respond.

Finally, after a long silence they say, "Well, Syb, let's just say there's more to us than meets the eye."

And with that, they take a long, big bite of a waffle and sit back even deeper into the woodland chair they seem to fit so comfortably in.

Chapter XXV

o o o

I guess it's time we tear down your notion that you don't have access to your mind, Syb. This one's a hard pill to swallow, so bear with me as we skip down the wild corridors of something else that's going to blow your mind. Perhaps you should have a seat and eat some of these goodies before we get into it." Ti points at a small mound next to them and I sit cross-legged, reaching out for a particularly fragrant chive and blueberry scone.

There is a tiny army of crumbs marching toward their freedom and claiming their independence on the delicate mantle of Ti's golden bib. Every so often, when Ti uses a delicately strong hand to make a point in their conversation, some of these crumbs succumb to a dishonorable death onto the dirt floor below. I find it hard to keep my mind focused on everything that Ti is telling me, so the entertaining exploits of these minute baked pieces keep me company as, indeed, my mind is being blown by everything I am hearing.

"Okay Syb, listen, all that hogwash of you being in a state of Non-mental activity at night is just that, absolute hogwash."

I gulp hard. How many times had I heard Mr. Wilhelm tell me that when I slept there was nothing in me, absolutely nothing that could be recognized as a thought, as anything true or reliable or even close to resembling something that I could trust? How many times had he told me, solemnly, with that wooden voice of his, that I should never, ever pay attention to anything that happened in my sleep?

The clash of my previously learned notions being bashed up by everything that Ti is telling me is leaving me deafeningly confused. I am having a hard time knowing who to trust anymore. And yet, the more Ti speaks, the more I feel their words pointing to something that I too have always known deep inside me but had never even dared whisper into the world for fear that I might do something that could break the perfect space that surrounded me.

Come to think of it, everything at the Company felt fragile that way. It felt propped up, like any gust of wind might send it toppling over, as if it were held up by strings and barely capable of keeping itself together.

I look over at Ti, who is looking intently at me. Although my throat is dry and tight, I muster up the courage and say, "Tell me more."

Something in Ti's body changes subtly. Their spine is more erect, there is a regalness to their chest, their voice does not frolic in the vowels and consonants as before, but instead meets my request with forthrightness and a drier tongue.

"Yes Syb, gladly. I know you've been trained to believe that there is nothing going on in that precious little head of yours, that it is like a blank space where nothing of your own volition could ever be produced. You've even been trained to think that you should be quite terrified of anything unusual ever showing up in there. It's an amazing thing, fear is. It can become a powerful weapon that keeps us at the very edge of what lies inside us. Wield it artfully, and fear can make everyone around you succumb into a quasi-idiotic stupor. But let me tell you Syb, and let me tell you very clearly, there is nothing to fear inside of you."

With this, Ti's eyes hold me in their golden gaze. The import of the words is slowly stitching itself into my insides, weaving itself in and out of me as the morning breeze ruffles some leaves behind me.

After another moment's pause, Ti continues, "There's a lot more inside you than meets the eye, Syb. I know you know that too, otherwise you wouldn't be here. I know that this information may shock you, but I also know that something within you knows that this is what you've been saying to yourself all along. I want to make something else extremely clear now: I am not saying anything you don't know already. That you've forgotten or gotten confused is one thing, but all of this you are hearing now is something you have known your entire life. I'm just here to remind you, that's all."

A delectable rush, like a sumptuous electric shock, runs down my spine and gallops through my arms and fingers. As I sit there, awash in the recognition that Ti's words are bringing to me, a memory crosses my mind and I ask, "Ti, that night, the night I woke up howling in my room with Bella. I was touching this wasn't I?"

Ti nods and I say, "But I know that it wasn't just me there. I am almost certain you were there too. I know I'm right."

A skinny, sexy grin ripples through the imperial cheeks and Ti says, "As I said to you before, I tried so many times to pop into that thick skull of yours but man, they had you on so many meds, it's a wonder you can even remember that at all. Yes, that was definitely me. I was trying to let you in on this little secret that you now know. Been trying to for years, actually. Tried it on one of your Streams too!"

A whoop and holler rocket out of Ti's mouth and I am catapulted into a memory of Ti at my threshold, of the mantle, of the goby fish, the smell of chrysanthemums, and of me about to fit into a shoe.

"You rascal!" I blurt. "That was you! You got me into so much trouble, Ti! Mr. Grim nearly had an aneurism when you appeared!"

Ti beams and chuckles contentedly, resting back into their woodland seat for a moment and says, "Ah...good times, good times."

"But what about the rest of it, Ti? The rest of it I really don't get. In my images, there is so much going on in there that I don't understand at all. All I can remember is this vivid sensation of my body being so...so...so alive!" This last word emerges out of me luminously, as if shining of its own accord and sits, poised, on my lips for me to enjoy its vitality and splendor.

"Well, about that," Ti begins, "that is something I know only a small glimmer of because this truly belongs to you, Syb. What I mean by that is, those are your own thoughts, your own inner landscapes coming through. But what I can share is that there is something deeply unusual about your particular images that attracted my attention and that still remains a mystery to me. For that, I'd need to fill you in a bit more on what you already know about Magdalena."

A crow flies overhead and caws out its poignant call into the open sky above us as Ti goes on, "Ah Maggie…what a gal. She was a special one. And well, what happened to her is what often happens to special people in this world.

"Maggie was found when she was pretty young, just like you, by Walt. He found her on the street, shivering, lost. I wish you could have met Walt back then, Syb. He was a very kind and sweet man, full of hope and what appeared to be an endless amount of energy that he could put into anything he was passionate about. When he saw Maggie shaking and shivering like that, his heart melted for her. It was instant. He fell in love with that girl and swore to do anything and everything for her.

"He took her in, fed her, bathed her, massaged her body back to health and then, when she was ready to speak, would listen to her for hours on end. To say that he was devoted to her is an understatement. Maggie had never received so much tenderness in her life. She too watched herself blossom towards him in ways she could never have imagined. What transpired between them is something few people get to experience in their lifetime. Not even the best Stream with its fairy tale romance motifs could stand a chance when compared to the love that these two shared. So intoxicating was the love between them that the air around them was always thick with the smell of fresh jasmine blossoms and sticky with the sweetness of molasses.

"The idea of the Dreammakers was still pretty new at that time and, once Maggie was back to health, Walt invited her to join him. He showed her, in his words, how much the people around her suffered, how intolerably uncontrolled their minds were, how much they needed someone to save them. When he invited Maggie to join him, he envisioned them both serving the people around them, heroically offering their time and lives to better humanity.

"Maggie was smitten and completely on board. They began going deeper and deeper, gathering information from Extractions, even writing scripts together and putting on Stream after Stream. Their work exploded onto the Network with the power of a thunderbolt. The honesty and rawness of Maggie's sincerity touched Consumers across thousands of homes and the effect was astounding.

"Walt would beam at Maggie with the deepest of prides as her Stream poured into living rooms, inundating those little Consumer habitats with her endless charm and intoxicating charisma. In Walt's own words, he would say that Maggie had been what he had always been waiting for and that, together, they were going to create the perfect world.

"Much time went by like this until, one day, Maggie was preparing for one of her regular Streams. This was standard procedure and, with Walt by her side, they both beamed in satisfied delight as she was plugged in.

"You might find it interesting to note that Maggie was in the midst of the Stream you just exited out of."

I look at Ti in surprise, "You mean Blanchette's story? The one with the hunter and the wolf?"

"Yep, that's the one. A particularly crafty Stream and script there, Syb. It took Walt ages to put that one together. It is my understanding that this particular script was a hard one to write because of the material Magdalena had given Walt to work with. Something about the content of Magdalena's mind had really stuck to Walt's teeth and he had a hard time chewing it up, making it digestible. He was nearly driving himself crazy trying to, as he said, 'clean up what he'd found in there'. But, he did, and he came up with the most kosher and aseptic version of her insides as he could create. This particular Stream took the Network by storm and was the biggest hit they had ever created. Consumers sat in their seats, mesmerized, enthralled, gulping the story in by the bucketloads, letting themselves simmer in the vivid images, steeping themselves in the thick moral stew of Walt's best creation."

I am quite surprised and find my interest increasing by the second. All of a sudden, I am blurting out, "It happened in that Stream, didn't it? It happened when she got to the woods. She got there, right to the spot where the wild rose bushes grow and she could not do it anymore. She heard the lines from the script, the lines her Mother had told her about Good Girls following the rules, but something in her just did not want to do it anymore. She got to the edge of the woods and could feel the Director coaxing her on, but something in her wanted to run away, to see what was behind the thin veil of the wood's edge, to see it for herself. That's why that Stream was such a disaster, wasn't it?"

Ti is looking at me, slightly astonished, their anemone eyes blinking brightly, and says, "Yes, quite right you are."

The words now burble and erupt of their own accord, they are a livewire river bubbling out of me, "And she managed to finish the Stream, but when she came back she was not the same. She knew she could not keep hiding from whatever lay within her. She knew she could not lie about it. She had to know, directly, from her own experience about that which the Director was so insistent was Bad and Evil and polluting the world. She could not keep hiding and pretending that this did not exist inside herself. She knew she could not face him, that's why she went into a coma. It was almost too much for her to know this about herself and face him."

At this, Ti becomes quite solemn and nods a serious nod. "Yes, quite so, Syb. You are right on the money."

The space between us is pierced again by the sound of the crow who has perched its dark, winged body on a branch above us. It is cawing once more while cocking its head and catching my eye with its mysteriously wild, yellow stare.

Ti's voice, like a jasmine bloom, then says, "To say that Walt was distraught is to pay a disservice to his loyalty. He was in shambles, cooing and wooing Maggie to come back to him. He had her in his office and had a cot set up next to her so that he could watch her every breath, her every moment of untouchable silence. His space was in disarray, he stopped bathing himself, he even stopped eating, such was his devotion to never leave her side.

I again find myself taking the reins of our conversation and know not where these words are coming from, but my voice is blooming out of me like a long cascade of wild flowers, "She came back for him. She came back but with a new voice, a new side of her, a part of her that she had never shared with him before. She wanted to offer it to him in the sacred place of their meeting, to place it on the shrine of their exchange, to ask him to love this part of her too. That was the yowl, the sound beckoning him to join her into a deeper love, a love that could transverse the strange lands of wild foxtails and loon wail, of eel song and snail dirge, of that which he had deemed uncouth, unholy, unfit to be seen. She was asking him to love her not only in that which was Good and Perfect and Nice, but all of her, including everything that had been exiled and put away into the dusty shadows of what could not be welcomed."

The crow above us flaps its wings, and I continue, "Love is a strange tapestry made of many unusual and unexpected threads. At times it will ask for sacrifice, and then demand infinite independence. It will clamor for valor and then require demureness. It will insist on communion but thrives on the profane. It aches for vitality but finds its profundity in the recesses of death. To answer the call to love is never a path that can claim to be known or familiar. One has to traverse the stormy sea of humility and never stop listening attentively. When the Director heard the call from love, he answered the only way he knew how."

Ti takes up the thread, "When Walt wheeled Maggie into the Extraction unit, it was the most profound expression of love he could call on. He wanted to know her, all of her. And when the Visibility Screen came on, the images toppled into the room like a feral cat, making a mess of the place and leaving behind them the stench of wild animal and pungent musk. One has to be very valiant to gaze upon all of our beloved and not look away. And valorous he was, as he gazed upon the scenes on the screen - the dark wooden landscape, the images of heavy footsteps, the dimly lit hut, the blood on the table - he uttered words that had a heartbeat of their own, they were pregnant with vitality and stuck to the walls like voracious ivy. He heavily muttered under his breath, 'Fox Woman dreaming.'"

As I hear these words, a deep shudder runs down my spine. The sounds cradle themselves between my vertebrae and whisper into my muscles, hugging themselves to my synapses. I know these words intimately. They make their way through my marrow and land, finally, in the living room of my belly button, taking residence there and putting up a sign on my insides, "Home, sweet home."

There is a long pause. The story is adrift on the waves of quietude. But then, Ti continues in measured tones, "The scalpel might be seen as a weapon," I find the courage to then add, "But in the hands of the Director, it was his way of loving Magdalena."

In unison, we both continue, "When he made the first incision, it was the language of care and affection that he was speaking. When the Visibility Screen did not falter but delivered the same images back, the second and third cuts were adoration. The fourth and the fifth were his manifest tenderness. The sixth and seventh were his pure reverence and devotion. The eighth and ninth were the purity of his passion. The tenth and eleventh were filled with ardor. When the Visibility Screen appeared more blurred and chaotic, but still conveying the same vehement images - the vermilion frizz, the wild stare, the deep verdant woods - the last cut, with his eyes drenched in tears, was his way to worship.

And, when the Visibility Screen finally went black, his last words to her were, 'This is how I can love you.'"

Chapter XXVI

o o o

The night has made its way through the forest, creeping and crawling its way through branches and twigs with its inky black hands, leaving its mark on everything it touches. The space around us is inundated with its dark luminosity. I find that I am exhausted and the moss invites me into its herbaceous embrace. I curl up into myself, take a look at Ti as they too are starting to gently close their giant, octopus eyes, and fall fast asleep.

Bramble. I am in the thicket of wild rose and honey locust bark. The thorny web of barbs is no longer a surprise to me and, instead of resisting them, I allow my body to become immediately soft and, soon, I am out of the net and close to the ground.

My attention is on the soil beneath me as it touches my body. It is slightly wet and the texture is mesmerizing, hypnotic in its unapologetic sincerity. The smell of the wet mud allows me to contrast it to my own smell, which I am now acutely aware of. It is rich, tart and strong and fills the space around me.

I know he is coming. I know it before my senses can recognize him. His body has left a watermark inside me that I know now from a distance. It is not long before his sonorous footsteps fill the night air with their cacophony.

I am by the window again. This time I am straining to see his every movement, memorizing his motions, wanting to intoxicate myself in the brusque dance of his strong hands and powerful arms.

It is irresistible, I long for him in ways so destructive my core trembles and shudders in the cold midnight air. He looks up, I look at him. Time becomes a solid, heavy object between our black pupils. I cannot resist it, although I should hide, I want him to find me. I beckon him, I beckon him.

Chapter XXVII

o o o

The loud yowl pierces the morning like an arrow. I am startled but also playfully entertained by the sonorous wake up call.

"Quite the alarm clock you got going on there, Syb." Ti is rubbing the sleep out of their eyes and picking at the small acorns that have gotten tangled in their wild, voluptuously wiry hair.

"I guess I should get used to this now," I say and squeeze out a smile, even though my face is still not fully awake.

"You mean get used to the fact that there is a whole world inside you and that you have full access to it all the time now? Or the howling yourself back into the morning?" Ti asks mischievously.

"Both." I reply. My grin is now fully roused and, much to my surprise, I find my whole body to be vibrant in ways I have never known before.

"It's the medication," says Ti, reading my mind again, "it's finally starting to wear off. You'll be back to yourself in no time at this rate."

I ponder on these words and say, "Ti, I have no idea what that means though, 'back to myself.' I don't know if I've ever even been myself." I pause, "What exactly am I going back to?"

Ti gives me a loving gaze and nods thoughtfully. "Well Syb, that's exactly what we're here to find out."

A butterfly flies by with the most graceful of motions, stopping every so often on small budding flowers and bouncing delicately on thin boughs.

I speak up again and say, "Ti, I keep meaning to ask. You've mentioned some other people from time to time, people who know your name, people whom you've met in the forest. Who are they? Where are they?"

"Ah Syb, you're one smart cookie, aren't you? Nothing gets past that little noggin of yours, huh?" Ti is pulling at a particularly entangled acorn and goes on, "Those folks, you ask. Well, how about we have ourselves a nice tall glass of orange juice and I'll tell you all about them."

With that, Ti produces a flask and two cups from the endless cornucopia that is their robe and pours us both a full glass of juice. As they do so, the sun peeks through the treetops and pours down in tangerine beams so that the whole morning is enveloped in citrus hues.

After taking a full gulp and sighing contentedly, Ti is making a comfortable seat for themselves on the leafy ground and begins, "Those folks...well, Syb, I have to let you know that you're not the first to crawl through that bramble hedge over there." Ti nods in the direction of the thorny wall that separates us from a time and space that feels almost foreign and incomprehensible to me now. "There have been many before you and probably many more will come after. They are other people who have decided to exit the story that they were living, inspired by curiosity, discontentment, hope or boredom. There are so many reasons people decide to wake up to themselves. You never fully know what spurs anyone to do it but, once in a while, they do."

I take a sip of my juice and contemplate what I have heard.

I ask, "And these people, where are they now? How come I haven't seen any of them?"

Ti folds their pearly hands over each other and answers, "They've all wandered off into the woods there." Again another nod, this time in the direction of the dimly lit bosk. "There are some of them who have chosen to live together, others who have chosen to ramble around on their own. Some who choose to spend half their time with people and half their time alone. You should see them, Syb. Most of them have decided to leave all clothes behind and wander around naked amongst the lichen and the brush. Many of them have stopped speaking, some only speak in onomatopoeic exclamations, and others choose to speak the language of the beetle, the frog and the duck. Still others speak in poetic prose or metered couplets and discourse extensively on the things they have seen, the things they have learned.

"They live among the trees and have become well acquainted with the song of the seasons, the anthems of the wind. Many of them know the dance of the cougar and others rhumba with the muskrat and the moles. Some have become so still, moss itself has confused them for rocks. And others, others are so lively and sleek that the river comes to them to cavort and frolic as the evening falls. They have all chosen a life among the dark, mysterious land of the woodland, Syb."

Ti's voice rocks back and forth between their cheek

and tongue, intoxicated by the images it has spoken.

It takes a while for me to speak, but eventually my curiosity eggs me on, "And these people, they were all Consumers at some point?"

Ti takes a moment and then nods once more, "Yes, yes they were. That's what's interesting about you, Syb. Maggie would have been the only other Dreammaker to want to come over and check out what was on the other side of the hedge but well, we know what happened to her…" A pregnant pause, and then, "So, you're the first Dreammaker to visit us on this side of the world."

I find this information shocking and struggle to make sense of it.

Ti looks at me sternly for a moment and says, "Now Syb, I just want to make something very clear here: that doesn't make you special. You need to know that. It's damn interesting, that's for sure, but it's not extraordinary. You're not made of any special stuff. Your story is not unrepeatable. The only difference between you and someone who chooses to stay glued to their Stream Screen and their regulated experience is that you chose to see what else was out there, what other options there could be. You might say you were too darned curious to keep yourself in the status quo. But that's nothing exceptional or rare."

I notice my heart is sinking a little. A part of me had come to think that these past days had some kind of uncommon tenor to them, some aspect of them that stood out of the ordinariness of everyday life.

Ti notices my countenance dropping and adds, "Syb, you gotta understand, this is good news. I know the Company fed you all kinds of stories about how special you are, about living the Princess life and how remarkable and important that is. You've fallen into believing that there is something innately different about you and that it sets you apart from others. That makes for a great divide between yourself and everyone around you, Syb. Realizing that you are not special means that you are no different from your average Consumer. On the contrary, you are incredibly close to each and every one of them because you are made up of the same bizarre thing that makes all of us tick. Think about it. This is deep, Syb, real deep." Ti gives me a meaningful look and, dropping their voice a bit, says, "It means that everyone can choose to wake up too if they so choose."

The butterfly I had been looking at earlier takes a magenta flight and disappears into the turquoise sky above me.

Ti also watches the watercolor wings wander and wane and then says, "This also levels out the playing field. You, me, a Teller, a Consumer, even good ol' Walt, we've all got the same things going on inside us. We've all got the opportunity to choose to walk a different path. It means no one is special, and everyone is special. It's great news, Syb, cheer up."

The thing about beliefs is that they seem to hold some kind of gravity to them, as if they were made of something other than the invisible threads of thought. The belief that I was special is woven inside me tightly and Ti's words threaten this delicate weft and I am scared of what may lay beyond it.

Ti swoops in immediately, "Ah yes, we've all had to deal with that. I know it hurts, I know it feels like there will be no one behind that idea of your specialness, that concept of your so called youness. Don't worry, Syb. Once you start free falling into this, you're going to grow to love it and, soon enough, you won't be able to get enough of it."

I let Ti's words wiggle their way into me and allow them to slowly take residence in the unquestioned territories of my insides.

Then another thought, rampant and galloping, comes bursting onto the scene. I say, "Ti, has anyone gone back?"

Ti looks at me quizzically, raising one of their fantastically groomed eyebrows, "Gone back?" They repeat.

"Yes," I say, "Has anyone who has come over the bramble and spent time in the woods, talking to ducks and whispering to frogs or whatnot, have any of them ever gone back to the Capital, back to their families, back to see what they left behind?"

Ti blinks blankly for a moment and says, "No, actually, I don't believe anyone ever has. The closest I can say anyone has ever done something like that was me popping up in your Streams or appearing randomly during people's sleep. But that's as close as it gets. And I only do that when I have an inkling that someone is really close and just needs a gentle nudge."

A part of me gets ignited and I find something boiling to the surface, "You mean no one has ever thought to go back and tell others about what there is beyond the din of ordinary life? No one has thought to unplug people from the Stream Screen and wake them the hell up? Are you telling me that they are just left there, expected to be okay with their lives as they are, oblivious to the rest of what is going on?"

Ti seems to be taking me in, sizing me up, measuring their words with the calm of someone who knows how to handle eruptions well. They respond, "Syb, now listen to me, I know this will probably come as a surprise to you and it will most likely shock your little system into overdrive so I want to say this as calmly as I can." Ti's voice is like custard now, thick and sweet as it drips on, "Most people, Syb, most people don't want to wake up."

I gulp, Ti continues, "In my experience, only those who want to wake up, do so. It's just like that. Even if you ran around with a sign pointing to the exit, most people would ignore you, call you crazy, exile you or, even more bizarrely, sacrifice you. It's funny that way."

Ti's eyes, dark and deep as the wood at night, stare at me from that strange place that they swim in. They say, "I know you're used to being in a story, Syb, dear. I know you're used to having princes and princesses, heroes that are doing good, and clearly delineated evil-doers that are meant to be stopped, etcetera. Look, I get it. It's easier to think of the world in terms of black and white. There is something very calming about the fairy tale narrative where you can clearly point out who the good guy is and who the bad guy is. Two very clearly different people, well-defined and completely opposite to each other." Ti seems to suppress a snigger. "It lets us sleep better at night. Makes everything feel nice and cozy inside us. Yeah, it does. Especially if you've decided that you're the 'Good Guy'".

Ti stifles another giggle and then continues, "Maybe you've even gotten it into that sweet little noodle of yours

that Walt and the Company are…uuu…dare I say it?…
Bad.¨

Ti can't seem to hold themselves together anymore
and is now fully chuckling and going red in the face as I sit
there, slightly bothered by the whole delivery and waiting for
the point to be made. We are quite the scene and the
morning watches on in merry delight.

¨Sorry, Syb. This is just too darned funny.¨ A last
little wheeze pops out of the grapefruit lips and takes a dive
straight into the orange juice flask.

¨Okay, okay. Gosh, that's just so darned entertaining,
really. But anyway, as I was saying,¨ Ti's face attempts to
contort itself, rather absurdly, into seriousness and goes on,
¨I really do get it, Syb. Believe me, I do. I had to figure this
out for myself a while ago. And, you know, from being
around the block a bit, I can tell you that things are a lot
more gray than they seem. I mean, sorry to break it to you
Syb but, in a way, if you check, you've got a lot of Walt in
you right now.¨ The millipede eyebrows go up, Ti's eyes
widen and stare at me in their Milky Way fashion, then says,
¨We've all got a bit of everything inside us. That's kinda the
point.¨

There's a moment's pause, the morning looks on
with contented enthusiasm and Ti adds, ¨Look, I'll be
honest with you, probably a part of you wants to play some

kind of role here, some kind of heroic savior thing of a sort. Before you run off and do all of that, I'll just give you a heads up: it ain't gonna work."

As Ti pauses for another breath, they appear to be taking me in again. They cock their imperial head a bit and add, "But, you know what Syb, don't take my word for it. You're gonna do what you're gonna do. The only way for you to figure this out is for you to do it yourself."

And with that, Ti takes a big swig of the wheeze-infused orange juice and then burps contentedly, staring off into the now celeste sky above.

Chapter XXVIII

o o o

The night has crawled out of its lair and slowly stretched its dark body over the space between us. Ti is lying prone, unmoving, having been silent for a long time now. I am fidgeting and moving madly, cracking twigs and rustling leaves beneath me with every motion.

There is something different about me this evening. Some form of restlessness is inhabiting my bones and the evening is pregnant with the feeling of change. I am aware that I am at the cusp of something new, but I know not what it is.

After an endless time of me jostling and wiggling, my exhausted body finally gives in, and I am immediately swallowed by sleep's wide, black mouth.

Bramble. I am in a thicket of wild roses and honey locust bark. This time, it does not surprise me. Instead, I feel endlessly at ease in the midst of this prickly landscape. Not a single thorn scratches me as I slowly shimmy my body down to the ground and land on my four feet.

My vision is clearer than ever before. My eyes are agile and perceptive, they are alert and awake. I find them scanning my surroundings with curiosity, taking in the taupe browns of the oak bark, the emerald greens of the maple leaf, the black shadows of the undergrowth.

And, as I become accustomed to the dimly lit terrain, my curiosity makes my eyes shift from the space around me to the body I inhabit.

I look down to find a furry coat meet me with its vivacious, auburn and rusty hues. My body is covered in a delicate, soft, hazel fur. There is a luminous agility that is exuded from my muscle and tissue, as if my body were forged of some instinctual intelligence and earthly brilliance. I see my paws touch the earth beneath me with perfect weight, as if the mud below me and the edges of my skin were intimately woven in material intimacy. I catch a glimpse of my white tail flicker like tiny lightning at the edge of my sight and, although I cannot see them, I can feel my ears twitch and move, welcoming the audible soundscape of the woods around me.

It is my ears that first catch a glimpse of him. This time, I can distinguish his particular timbre with the precision that only familiarity can bring. I then catch sight of him, his large body a shadow at first, and then a muscular figure making its way back into his softly illuminated hut.

I follow him, crouching as I always have at the edge of the window, just outside his line of vision. I am intoxicated immediately. His movements are gruff and terse and my body sways in the rough tune of his choppy motions. I ache to be in his calloused hands, cut into pieces, devoured too. I yearn to come close to his fragrant body and devour him too, bit by bit, in slow nibbles and voracious bites. I ache to mix my body with his and have his own musculature and tendons blend with my soft tissues and wild bone.

And as the fire of my longing pulses through me, I find myself walking inside, into the warm walls of his hut, staring straight at him, walking with the delicate dance of both sacrifice and executioner and then laying down, on the table, directly under his knife.

Chapter XXIX

o o o

This time, the howl is a welcomed sound, and I could argue that I might have even been awake a moment before it emerged just to catch it in its entirety. It emerges loudly into the stillness of the morning and cavorts around us in clumsy excitement. I watch it bounce against the tree trunks, scattering a flock of sleeping blue jays and then see it dart off into the secret place where all sounds go to live the rest of their sonorous lives.

Ti too is not surprised by my morning sounds anymore and, instead, lets out a loud yawn. They then stretch the entirety of their golden-attired flamingo body and smack their lips happily, welcoming the morning with a cheery, "Howdy do!"

I smell it first. It is a smell I am so intimately close to, it seems strange that it should be coming from any other place than my own body. But there it is, a scent so heavy in its familiarity, so weighty in its odor that it creates an indentation in the soil beneath it.

Ti's nostrils, those delicate, dark pearls, are the next to notice its presence. They sniff the air with tiny, regal movements, curious and intrigued, trying to find the source of such a hefty scent.

I spot it first. It is lying close to my feet, almost touching me. The vermilion hue is the first thing to catch my eye. But it is the voltaic charge that buzzes around it that holds me magnetized to its shape.

Ti spots it too and appears to be glued to its inner electricity, its whirring charm.

A moment passes, then another, then a whole family of them parades by trying, unsuccessfully, to grab our attention by wearing carnivalesque paraphernalia and hooting and tooting as they go along. But it is to no avail. Both Ti and I are immobile, frozen by the appearance of this new shape in the space between us.

It takes a long time for either of us to speak and, when Ti finally clears their throat, the long procession of moments cheer in victorious glee.

"It, um, it looks like it's for you," Ti says, in a hoarse voice.

I emerge from the immobility I was in and give a small nod in recognition of the truth of what Ti has said.

In an instant, I know what to do.

I reach out for the shape at my feet and am met with the softest of textures, an almost liquid solidity that feels too familiar to explain. The tail, a lighting bolt of white, pours down the side of the still warm body and the eyes, although lifeless, stare at me from the dark, mysterious place of wonder and death.

A fox pelt. Not any fox pelt, my own fox pelt, the pelt of my dreams, the pelt that is me.

Again, as if instructed by some unknown force, I find my hands moving in a choreography of perfect intelligence. I place the head directly above my own, the mouth hanging over my forehead like a peculiar set of wild bangs. Its spine cascades down my own bony vertebrae, with the tail hanging directly below my lower back, and the front paws tie around my neck, holding my body and this wild creature in close embrace.

It is then that I look at Ti and Ti looks silently, solemnly, back at me.

"You know what I have to do now, don't you?" I ask, my voice a timbre I have never heard before, as if possessing its own powerful heartbeat, as if full to the very edges of the vitality of its sonority.

For the first time in these past four days, a small shadow crosses Ti's face, the faintest murmur of sadness passing through their otherwise always brilliant countenance.

¨Yes, Syb, I know.¨

We get up and wipe off the leaf debris that has stuck to us overnight. Ti walks me to the edge of the bramble, each of our footsteps thoughtfully placed. The silence between us is laden with knowing.

When we arrive to the spot that I emerged from, Ti turns to me and places both of their ivory hands on my shoulders.

¨I have to say, Syb, I am quite pleasantly surprised. It's not that I ever know what anyone is ever going to do. No, never. I told you at the very beginning of our meeting, we were in a liminal place, we were sitting in the great I Don't Know and I would never pretend to assume to know what will come next. That's what's so fun about all of this. But people become kinda predictable after a while, you know. It's not that it's never exciting, but it's hardly ever surprising. And you, well, you're a piece of work, Syb.

Thanks for shaking me out of my own tiny complacency. Thanks for reminding me of what I came to remind you of."

Ti pulls me close to them and the feeling of their body close to mine is as inexplicable as every other part of them. I am held in the warmest of embraces, ferociously squeezed in the most delicate of touches, and steadily held in a feather-soft, enveloping hug.

When we pull apart, Ti finishes by saying, "Thanks for the fun, Syb. I've had a blast. Hope you have too. See you when I see you."

And with that, I am down on my hands and knees, slowly making my way through the bramble and the thorns, headed right back to the place I came from.

Chapter XXX

o o o

I have become skilled in dodging thorns and my journey through the bramble leaves me unscathed. I emerge back into the well lit edge of the woods and catch a glimpse of the familiar wild rose bushes that catalyzed the last few days into existence.

I am back on my feet as I look upon the sunny scene before me. It is exactly as I left it.

I make my way toward the cobblestone street and start walking back into town.

At first, the sound is muffled, as if trying to burst through a thick wall or pounding its way through a condensed space. I am unable to locate its source. It seems to come from somewhere distant, as if attempting to emerge from the clouds and sky above me.

As I get closer and closer to the center of town, the place that I called my home in my Stream, the place where the woman who played my mother lived, the voice becomes blaringly loud and, although I still cannot make out the words it is saying, the hostile undertones fill the air around me.

As I open the door and smell the familiar scent of lavender scones, I look around me and find no one there. And, come to think of it, no one was on the streets either. The whole place feels abandoned.

Once I am inside, unsure of exactly what I am looking for, but knowing full well that I am exactly where I need to be, the voice becomes clearer and louder. I raise my head as if trying to find the source and finally make out a whole sentence.

"Wretch! Wretch! You have to fix this immediately, you filthy miscreant you!"

I make out the voice to be the Director's. The sound is bulging with tension, its veins popping out with stress. I stand still and listen on intently.

"Sybil! Sybil! You get your act together now, you fool of a woman. We've been live this whole time. Everyone is watching! Do you realize what you've done? Do you even understand the severity of your actions, the level of horror and pandemonium you have brought upon everyone? They trusted you, Sybil. The Consumers trusted you with their lives, with their Morality, with their sense of what is Good and Correct and were depending on you to show them how to live Good Lives. Now you've destroyed all that for them. You need to fix this immediately, Sybil. Get back on the script now!"

I listen and let the sounds wash upon my shores. I let them ebb and flow in an almost detached manner, knowing full well that they have no power over me.

"Sybil! Sybil, are you even listening to me? Do you even remotely understand what you have done? I'm ordering you to fix this now. Get back on the script. We are going to correct all of the mess you've made right this instant. Sybil!"

It is at that moment that I feel the cold, tangy outline of the Bridgepiece in my hand. Its cold contours feel strangely obscene when held against the soft warmth of my skin. Its latent power gives it a liveliness of its own, as if it could suddenly burst into life. It feels strangely alien to me.

Then, all at once, I know what I have to do.

I walk to the middle of the room where the blazing hearth sits nonchalantly and unexpectant. Having known itself only to be a piece of the scenery, never a main protagonist, it sits in its demure role as background object and barely even notices me as I walk closer and closer to its flaming mouth.

It happens in a second, as all things do. I half expect the moment to stretch out, to expand itself, to let more of time seep through its drawn out edges. But no, the moment lasts as long as any other moment does and, in it, I have let go of the Bridgepiece and sent it straight into the middle of the billowing fire.

Above and around me comes a strange wail and then the sound of static gone drunk. I hear the retreating sound of the Director's voice yelling words I cannot make out anymore and then, quiet.

The house is filled with complete, utter, palpable quiet. Even the objects around me have become still and hushed.

A wave of electricity passes through me, leaving in its wake the sensation of pure lucidity.

And then I hear my voice, rotund, grave, inhabited from within itself say, "Listen, Sybil. Listen to the sound of your own voice. Anchor there. Listen. Wake up. Wake up!"

Chapter XXXI

o o o

I am in the Office. I smell of musk and old bougainvillea petals. I can also detect the aroma of ripe pear and magnolia fields dancing in the undertones of my scent. My naked body is slightly sticky on the leather chair that I have laid in so many times before. I feel the familiar tendrils of the Media Outlet adhered to my forehead and I slowly allow my heavy eyelids to open and close over and over again until I can make out the shapes before me.

Anne's face is the first one to come into focus. Her normally pudgy and amicable countenance is red and nervous. A thin stream of cold sweat is making sticky dance moves in rivulets on her blotchy forehead. She is standing behind a chair, wringing her hands nervously over and over again, muttering under her breath, "Sugar and spice and everything nice, that's what little girls are made of. Sugar and spice and everything nice…"

Bella is beside her. Unlike Anne, who is fidgeting incessantly, Bella is cold, immovable, her eyes transfixed on me. Actually, not on me particularly, but on the pelt that lies atop my head. She seems to be hypnotized by the fox's fangs and incapable of moving.

As I blink a couple more times, the faces of Jacob and Wilhelm, stony, implacable, like marble in their impenetrable state, also come into focus. They are standing beside Bella and Anne, holding clip boards and pens in midair. They too seem to be transfixed and unmoving.

The last face to come into focus is the Director's. Odd that it is the last one that I can make out since he is quite literally hovering above me, his face just inches away from mine. I can make out the smell of his candy cane perfume now and I see the small veins in his eyes rioting and going on a rampage as he stares, unblinkingly at me.

Since no-one seems to be moving or saying anything, I decide to sit up straight, which causes my skin to rub up against the leather chair. It makes the most irreverent of noises in the midst of the tense room around me which makes me giggle, but the joke lands flat on its face for the rest of my audience.

I decide to remove the electric wires attached to me and, when I disconnect myself from the first electrode, this awakens the Director from his catatonic state. He yells out, sending a small army of tiny spit particles into the space around him.

"No! You are not disconnecting yourself, you hear me! We are going to fix this right now, Sybil. I don't care how long it takes or what we have to do, you are going to do as I say and we are going to fix this immediately. We are going back into your Stream and you are going to do everything I tell you to do. You have wreaked havoc and now you are going to clean up the mess you have made!"

Anne lets out a small, feeble snivel that runs around in circles at the edges of the room, trying to make itself invisible, until finally finding a mouse hole and scampering into it.

I turn and look at the Director unwaveringly. He returns my gaze and seems to take me in for the first time. His eyes are glued to my face and, without words, I point at the fox pelt surrounding me. It is then that, very slowly, unwillingly, he lays eyes on the furry raiment, the sharp teeth, the bright, beady eyes. I then guide his gaze to my hands and, unhurriedly, open them wide. He is met with the nakedness of my palms, the evidence of freedom, the undeniable mark of autonomy. He nervously looks back at the pelt, then back at my hands and then, once again, into my calm and fixed stare. The slow realization of me coming back from a Stream without a Bridgepiece makes his face ashen, it is like watching an eclipse of understanding make its way in slow motion over his red globe of a face.

The Director's demeanor changes. Where before his shoulders stood square and firm, they now droop and make him look old, defeated. His body slouches and his eyes sink deeply into their sockets. He looks at me plaintively and, almost sniffling, says, "The Consumers, Sybil. Think about them. Our poor, dear Consumers need us. Don't you understand? Without us showing them the way, they are completely lost. If we don't care for them, lead them down Correct paths, give them Good Models to follow, explain to them what is Right and what is Wrong, we are condemning them to endless suffering. I know you can't possibly want that. You don't want that, Sybil, I know you don't. I know you care for them, I know you want to save them too. Please Sybil, go back on, do it for them. We must save the Consumers."

I look at the man in front of me in a way that I never have before. I calmly rip off the rest of the tentacled wires and electrodes from my forehead, get off the chair and make my way to the door.

As I turn around and look back at him, I say, "No one ever needed to be saved, Walt.

With that, I walk out the door, make my way to the main entrance, and leave towards the sunny outside.

Chapter XXXII

o o o

The Office is heavy with shock. It stands there, holding itself up against its four walls, trying hard not to faint, doing its best to keep its stable structure of mortar and brick.

It is Anne who makes the first sound, a faint, forlorn monosyllable, perhaps the onomatopoeic soundtrack of confusion, perhaps the remnants of her previous snivel. It is making its way toward the Director, who catches it and then looks at her in bewilderment, unable to truly take her in, perhaps even incapable of knowing who she is at that moment.

She stutters, "Wh...what...what are we going to do now?"

Before the question mark has finished making its serpentine motion and being dotted at the bottom, the Director has haphazardly laid himself down into the chair and is pulling at the wires of the Media Outlet, placing them in their polkadot pattern on his aging head.

"I have to fix this, I have to fix it now..." The Director's voice fades quickly into silence as his eyes shut and the Stream Screen is filled to the brim with images.

Anne, Bella, Wilhelm and Jacob watch in astonished silence as a parade of candy, baked goods and rainbows fill the monitor, displaying the contents of the Director's inner world.

Slowly, the confectioner montage dissolves into the familiar hut that Sybil had just emerged from moments before. The Director has moved into Sybil's Stream and is now inhabiting it from within. The image of the loving mother appears on the screen, smiling beatifically, as scones are gently being piled into a basket. The sounds of birds chirping and happy neighbors pass by in succession, with the voices of people greeting each other and exchanging kind pleasantries as they go along.

The cobblestone street slowly starts to dissolve into a grassier path and, eventually, the image of the woods' edge starts to get closer and closer. As they come into focus, it appears as if the trees have been rendered innocuous, as if made hygienic and individually packaged. The grass on the floor appears to have been combed and blow dried into perfectly coiffed, green bouffants, and the moss on the rocks have been tailored so that not a single strand of them is frayed or out of place.

The woodlands appear on the screen as a cardboard scenery, immaculate and artificial, safe and completely inoffensive.

As the path opens up into a small clearing, something flashes on the screen, a streak of feral crimson, a whisper of the untamed.

The images halt for a moment and attention is returned to the path, to the harmlessness of the environment. Focus comes to the scones in the basket, to the sound of birds chirping. But the flash comes again, this time more vibrant, this time unignorable.

The sound of the Director's voice landing in crashing staccatos into the room makes everyone jump and look around in disbelief.

"Get it out of here, Wilhelm! Get it out!" the voice thunderously calls.

Wilhelm looks around bewildered, first trying to understand how the Director is speaking to them and then confused as to the meaning of the words themselves.

"Sss…sir?" He stammers out.

"Get it out of here, Wilhelm. Whatever that is. It cannot be here. We need to clean this whole damned place up. You need to remove it, Wilhelm. You need to get it out!" The Director's voice is making the whole Office shake under its intense insistency.

"Sir, I'm sorry but....how do I do that? What do you want me to do?" Wilhelm responds, doubtfully.

"Get the scalpel, Wilhelm. Get the scalpel and cut it out."

Wilhelm looks at Jacob with wide eyes and uncertain gaze. Jacob's empty stare back does nothing to reassure him. He is standing there, weighed down by the demand, feeling heavy under his thick suit and unable to move.

"Do as I say, Wilhelm!"

Under the pressure of the demand and after much hesitation, Wilhelm walks to the back of the room, pulls out his operating implements and makes his way back to the Director's dreaming body.

As he pulls on his gloves, he looks around the room again to get some form of support, some form of agreement, but Bella, Anne and Jacob can only stare at him in stunned disbelief.

On the screen, the verdant images of the woods still stand in their perfectly reliable verticality and, once again, the Director's voice storms into the Office saying, "What are you waiting for, Wilhelm? Do it!"

With a trembling hand, Wilhelm cleans the Director's head with a cotton wad and then pulls the bone saw and scalpel out of their casing.

The walls hold their breath as Wilhelm places the rough blade on skin and, with calculated pressure, makes the first cut.

The room is filled with the smell of organic matter, like the smell of a beet root crying or a rose delicately hemorrhaging. A small trickle of blood lands on the tiled floor, creating the inexplicable art that only living tincture knows how to make.

When the second cut is made, and the tiniest sliver of the Director's skull is removed, Wilhelm looks back up to the Screen, looking expectantly to see what has changed.

On the Screen, the woodlands have become more vibrant and strangely sweeter, as if dripping with sugar or made of hard candy. The image is odd and eerie but the cheery voice of the Director seems to think the contrary, "Yes Wilhelm! Yes, my boy! You did it. It's gone. It's gone!"

The Screen follows the grassy path and goes deeper into the woodlands and it is there that a flash of yellow eyes, a blaze of red fur quickly scurries through the undergrowth, disappearing as quickly as it had appeared.

Bella gasps and Anne reaches out for her hands. The two of them stand there, eyes glued to the Screen, captivated by the scene before them.

"Again!" The Director yells, "Do it again, Wilhelm! Cut more out. We have to remove this permanently, otherwise we will never be able to correct the damage that has been done. Cut, Wilhelm, cut!"

Again Wilhelm looks at Jacob and, this time, he is met with the shadow of sadness, a glimmer of defeat and then a nod, an acknowledgement, and the most anorexic of yeses one has ever heard.

The scalpel is against gray matter, the incision is quick, the content is removed and the Office again is filled with the sharp smell of exposed body.

On the Screen, the image is slightly more blurry, the edges less defined, but the Director's voice is euphoric and erupting, "Yes! Yes! You did it. This time it is most definitely gone, I know it is."

But the flash is undeniable, the fur is now recognizable, the eyes steadier in their beady wisdom and the crashing waves of the Director's disappointment tumble into the Office, chilling the marrow of those standing, watching.

"Again, Wilhelm, again!" The Director yells.

Scalpel against bone, incision against brow, Wilhelm cuts again and quickly looks up for signs of any progress.

"This…this must be it," Wilhelm stammers.

But it is not. The leaves' edges have become blurred and the previously clear path has now become a muddy bog. And again, the crimson hue, the furry dash, the wild pupil make their way through the monitor's sheer, black edges.

"Again, Wilhelm! Again! We have to remove this permanently, don't you see?! Do it again." Although the Director's voice is slightly slurred, its imperious demand is strong and implacable.

Another cut, and then another, and then another. But the images are relentless, over and over again the undomesticated flash of wildness streaks across the Screen, indomitable, unyielding.

As the woodlands transform into a mashup of haphazard greens and intoxicated browns, the Director's voice too suffers from imprecision and blurriness. The words are now gummy and they sloppily try to make their way into the Office. They are on their hands and knees, feebly attempting to articulate in imprecise language the same command.

"Again, Wilhelm, again. We must remove this permanently. They are all depending on us, the Consumers depend on us for everything. If we don't remove this, they are forever cursed into suffering. We have to save them from this. You must do it, Wilhelm, you must. Remove it from me, please, please just remove it…"

Wilhelm's eyes have become glazed. No longer are his movements shaky or trembling. A solid precision has taken over him, an icy clarity is guiding him now.

"Yes, indeed," Wilhelm replies, "I must remove this from you. This cannot stay as it is. Clearly this part of you is unfit to stay here. We have to clean this whole thing up." His voice is glassy too, emerging from the cold place where actions become commands and care is no longer considered.

The scalpel has now become an extension of his hands, the cuts are now mechanical. There is so little left, that this final cut, this final incision, lands in the very center of the Director's skull and then, from the Screen, nothing.

The blackest of voids stares out into the room, gaping in its ridicule of those who are still looking at it, those who are hoping for something other than what it is delivering. But the Screen is unkind and miserly in that way and all it gifts that cold Office is an image into dark oblivion.

Chapter XXXIII

o o o

Wilhelm is the first to move. The room is thick with biology and the floor is splattered with organic matter dancing its bizarre, liquid dance.

His footsteps ring dissonantly in the frigid echoes of the Office. He is once again in the back of the room, gathering new implements.

As he makes his way back to the chair, he brusquely grabs Jacob by the arm and hoarsely says, "I need your assistance for this."

Jacob walks awkwardly beside his brother as Anne and Bella stand, aghast, watching everything unfold before their astonished eyes.

Wilhelm places his instruments on a tray beside the chair, next to the Director's lifeless body, and instructs Jacob to put on gloves.

Wilhelm then pulls out a needle and thread as well as a large amount of cotton wads that he hands over to Jacob. "Place them where I tell you," Wilhelm instructs gruffly.

The first handful of cotton wads get stitched together into the Director's skull, then the second and third, as if they were stuffing a giant plush toy, until the entire head is put back together and moulded into shape.

As Wilhelm adds the finishing stitches that hold the whole thing together, Wilhelm orders, "Anne, Bella, get over here."

Wilhelm's voice commands the two of them into motion and they scuttle, reluctantly and in horror, to the Director's side.

"Bella, fix his hair. And Anne, use some of your makeup on him to bring some life into his face. We need him to look alive." Wilhelm is curt and clear, giving no place for either of them to doubt or question what they are doing.

Once they are done, Wilhelm reaches out for the needle again and sews the Director's eyelids open. Lastly, he strings his hands and elbows to long, sturdy cords and props him up to a seated position.

"Jacob," Wilhelm states, "we are going to do a different kind of Stream today. Go and stand behind the Screen, I'll need you to operate the Camera. You are going to point it at the Director in a moment and we are going to go live. Bella, Anne, you are going to sit beside the Director and smile as beatifically as you ever have. Give us your best Loving Mother and Princess look. I am writing you a script and you are to say everything I tell you to. Do you understand?"

No one moves or answers. Wilhelm, seeing all of them in quasi catatonia, lets out a loud sigh and then grunts in exasperation.

"Ugh…" An exasperated sigh peeks its steely head through his cold lips, "Look, just think of the Consumers, ok? They are going to need something to hold on to after all the chaos Sybil created. And even more after all this here mess…"

Wilhelm's eyes travel to the bloody contents in the room, then continues in exasperation, "The Consumers are too damned dumb to figure any of this out for themselves."

Another blank-stared silence meets Wilhelm's irritated grumbles.

He finishes with a flurry, "Just get to it."

Something in the words sounds hollow, as if lurking behind some twisted intention. However, unable to pinpoint what exactly lands oddly for them, the three begin to move in slow motion and do as Wilhelm says.

The three are now ready at their places as Wilhelm scribbles down a script that he hands to the women and then proceeds to sit behind the chair, holding the strings attached to the Director's hands and pulling them up and down, making the Director's body dance a strange, morbid dance.

Before ordering Jacob to go live, Wilhelm looks around the room at the three people standing awkwardly before him.

In a gruff voice he says, "The Company's work cannot stop, do you understand? I will continue Walt's legacy. After this, we will take up where we left off and resume all other Streams as if none of this ever happened. We will go back to our regular programming."

Wilhelm's voice drops and he then adds, "And, let me make myself completely clear, no one, not one of you can even breathe a word of what has happened here tonight. This is between us and us alone. If I even hear of one of you mentioning any of this to anyone, you are done. You hear me? Done."

He then turns to Jacob and says, "Start Streaming. We are going live."

Chapter XXXIV

o o o

X0720 had sat for the last four days propped up onto his now dead sofa. Packets of Evening Delights laid strewn across the floor and his chin glowed with phosphorescent cheese remnants as well as some incandescent oranges, while his eyes stared blankly ahead at the now black screen.

He had come home for his routine Tuning days and had been watching Sybil's Stream, glued to it in an incomprehensible way.

Something in him had been stirred when she had disappeared into the thicket of woods. Some long forgotten memories had emerged from deep within him. Some remote longing seemed to ache inside him. Had he had the words to pinpoint his experience, he could have said that, for a moment, a stir of rebellion, a flicker of dissent, had crossed his tame landscape. But these were not words that X0720 knew.

He instead chose to blame, once again, the expired food items he must have eaten, had carelessly disposed of any sense of personal considerations, and had rested his balding head back into the indented padding behind him.

When, however, the Screen had thrown these last images of woodland creatures, of flashing reds, of undomesticated eyes straight into his grey living room, it was hard for him to deny that something had crept into his mind and seemed to have taken hold of him.

It felt, he would have said had someone asked him, as if a distant knowing were whispering inside him. As if a sudden hint of the different, the unknown, were peeking its rascally head over the picket fence of his well-groomed mind. As if unasked, repressed questions were causing mischief in the attic of his disciplined interior. And, as if the vague feeling of discomfort with the status quo were trying to scratch its mangy fur in the well-vacuumed rooms of his domesticated soul.

Perhaps, had this been a man of a different temperament, a man with a different history, a man with a penchant for wonder, X0720 would have possibly turned off the Stream Screen and wrestled, danced and listened to the new flavors that were coloring his world. Perhaps he would have emerged from his small room and wandered the streets in search of answers. Perhaps he himself would have gone off to the edge of the woods, beckoned by the mystery, hungry for his own story.

But, alas, X0720 was not of that temperament, was not of that calling. X0720 was simply not that man.

And, perhaps, that is exactly what Wilhelm knew deep down inside him when he wrote his script and ordered Jacob to start the live Stream. Perhaps he knew that there were few out there who would have the call to adventure even after all they had witnessed, even after the undeniable lucidity they had seen delivered to them in the comfort of their own reliable homes.

Perhaps Wilhelm knew that most, if not all, of the Consumers that had just seen a full schism of their well constructed realities would simply rest back into their well-worn sofas, look straight ahead into their shiny Screens and wait, just wait, for another image that they could swallow, another predigested script that they could follow, another dream that they could drift into, eyes wide open, and fall asleep again. Just fall asleep.

Chapter XXXV

o o o

The Screen is filled with the smiling faces of Bella and Anne sitting on either side of the widely grinning Director. Although rarely seen live, all Consumers are familiar with the Director's warm, cheery face that is plastered all over the Capital's large billboards, as well as throughout the many commercial breaks that pepper Streams with alluring invitations to buy the latest Dreammaker doll, the newest Dreammaker's makeup kit, the most up-to-date list of what a Dreammaker is looking for in their ideal prince.

The Stream that is on the Screen now is not presented in the usual format of the regular broadcasting. But there are so many lively colors in the background, so many whimsical sounds every couple of seconds, so many close ups of Bella's inordinately beautiful face, that the uncharacteristic nature of it all soon slips by unnoticed.

Anne is merrily singing a song as the Director's hands clap and slap his thighs in syncopated rhythm. The camera never focuses on his face, so hardly anyone notices the strange fact that he never blinks and is staring, sullenly, at a fixed, invisible point before him. Or that his arms seem to be being moved by strings and not of his own accord. All of that fades away in the background.

Instead, the Consumer's attention is drawn to Bella's radiant face and pearly voice as she fills the Screen now. Her golden tresses grab hold of her audience as she delivers the final words of her long monologue, "And so, boys and girls, remember the lesson that our beloved Sybil has given all of us today. Sybil, who sacrificed herself for all of you because she loves you that much and wanted to show you how important it is to always do the Right thing. Remember, and remember well: never ever stray from the path of what is Good and Correct, or terrible, terrible things will happen to you."

Her wide grin and impossibly white teeth beam out of the Screen and impress the moral of the story on her adoring audience.

The image is now cutting to commercials and a parade of satin pinks, banana yellows and lemon greens is running around announcing the newest product on the market and, slowly, the Stream comes to an end.

Chapter XXXVI

o o o

I am outside. I am walking through the asphalt streets of the Capital's wide network of urban mazes and terrains. The Sun pours down on me in its honey rays, warm against my naked skin.

I have been walking for hours and have come across no one. The streets are empty but I can see from the many windows of the Consumer's housing units the flickering images of Stream Screens busily dancing in their frenzied jitter.

Much time passes like this until, finally, Consumers running their afternoon errands start pouring out and walking their robotic walks to the shops and stores around me.

I stand there, smiling, expecting them to recognize me. After all, I was the Dreammaker that had inhabited their living rooms and entered their tiny homes over and over again for many a Tuning Day.

As one dark-haired woman passes me by, I look her directly in the eye and think I see a glimmer of recognition. I expect her to stop and have a "Hello" ready and waiting between my lips. But, instead of a greeting, instead of recognition, she hastily quickens her steps and passes me without even a nod, a hint of acknowledgement.

I shrug it off thinking that perhaps she is in a hurry and look ahead at an elderly man who is also coming my way. I smile again and walk towards him. And again, I sense a brief moment of recognition that immediately gets replaced with a hastened step and he passes me by.

I look at a young woman and wave. She looks away and walks straight into the open door of a shop.

I greet a couple and say, "It's me. It's Sybil, the Dreammaker. I'm the one on your Screen, from the Company. You know me." But the couple seem not to have heard me and walk on, getting swallowed up by the now growing crowd.

I repeat this with a younger man, an elderly woman, a man carrying a package home, a pair of slender women, a well-dressed middle aged man, but no one stops. No one returns my greeting. They all walk by, leaving me unnoticed, standing there amidst the mass of people, perplexed, confused.

I make my way to the shops and walk inside, speaking to the women at the counters, the men at the cash registers. But to no avail, I am ignored just as equally.

I walk through large stores and small shops, through the phosphorescent aisles of the Refreshment Center and the intricate corridors of the boutique Beauty Shops. I meet as many people as I can but none of them return my smile, all of them stare past me as if I were not there.

Night comes and I nestle myself into a dark alley. A memory of a time when I had done this before flickers before me and, instead of shivering and pitiful, I gather myself up, surrounding myself with my pelt and rest contentedly, calm and carefree.

For two more days I roam the streets of the Capital, always with the same result until, finally, I have walked so far that I come to edge of the city.

"I guess it's time for another liminal dip then," I whisper mischievously to no one in particular.

I look back at the Capital one last time, gazing at the many Consumers making their way through the early morning to their varied destinations and, with one last quiet farewell, I turn and cross the asphalt threshold and am immediately embraced by the lively tendrils of wild grass and unruly weeds.

Chapter XXXVII

o o o

I have been living here for longer than I can remember. I stopped counting time once the Sun continued to set over and over again over my humble lodging. It seemed like a pointless task, counting days, watching time go by.

I found this hut some days after I left the Capital. I made my way through the woods and found an abandoned hunter's lodge, made of impeccable stone and reliable mortar.

I have made my home here and live in lively contentment, dressed in my beautiful grey mantle, listening to the sound of rain and moon, becoming deeply acquainted with the speech of loons, the giggle of hare, the raucous tantrums of toad.

Wild oregano is my friend and, as companions, I have the festive friendship of deer and quail, the thought-provoking presence of bear and cougar, and the reliable conversation of spruce and fir.

From time to time I visit the Capital, always aware of the invisible cloak that seems to surround me. I like sitting and watching the Consumers go by in their hasty pace and decided step. I like becoming familiar with their angular bodies and their shallow breath. I enjoy watching them tarry from time to time, a glimmer of a thought of change, a flicker of desire aroused within them. Then I simply sit and watch as that flicker fades away and quickened stride takes its place.

For so long I have done this that their faces are now familiar, they are etched in me in care. In a strange way, they are my family too, alongside the wild darlings that inhabit the wood.

I make my way from woodland to city, stitching myself back and forth between these two worlds, quilting them together, preferring neither and enjoying both.

It is dusk when I first perceive him. It is the dissonant sound of boot amidst the harmonious symphony of my marshy surroundings that gives him away.

I am inside my hut, a warm fire setting everything aglow, the heated orange of the hearth licking the contours of my walls with its sweltering tongues. The smells of an evening meal flirt tenderly through my earthen room, coquettishly wiggling through the cracks in the door and gleefully seducing their way into the night.

I can feel him spying on me through the window, the warmth of his body touching me even at a distance.

I can feel the way air moves through him, the way his marrow pulses with life, the enticing way his muscles hug closely to the delightful shape of his bones.

I turn slowly, letting my body become soft and pliable. As I look out my window and catch his own dark pupil, I can suddenly understand why it is that he can see me.

The clamor of freedom pulses through him like a potent lightning bolt. His ache for sovereignty throbs, almost knocking down the walls of my well-built home. He stands there salivating for the mystery, licking his lips for the unknown. And it is in that way that I realize what beckons us to each other, what makes us visible to the one who yearns to see, what inner calling brings us to the one who longs as well.

I walk to the door and open it wide, speaking both to him and to the night. My words spill out and land on the silvery backs of the stars mirrored in the mud and I say, "I've been waiting for you."

Epilogue

o o o

O nce upon a time, not long ago, in a forest not too distant from here, there was a hut.

The hut was inhabited by a simple man, a hunter, who spent his days and nights amidst the verdant clamor of the forest, looking for wild game and passing his lonely life coming and going from his stone home to the many places of the wild woods.

It happened on an eve like any other eve, an eve that would have never stood apart in its ordinariness and routine shape and form. And as nonchalant as this eve had begun, as it made its way into nightfall, this particular eve would stand out in this hunter's memory forevermore.

As he walked through the brush, making his way back after a long day of hunting, carrying the small bodies of two hares over his shoulder, he saw his hut flickering with the distinctive shade of orange that only a hearth ablaze can produce.

Suspicious, he walked silently to his door and looked in through the window only to find his fireplace alit and a warm bowl of soup, nonchalantly waiting for him, on his wooden table.

Confused, he made his way inside and, reserved at the beginning and then heartily enjoying it at the end, he ate the soup and, finding no one in the hut, finally made his way to bed and heavily slept the night away.

The next morning, he bolted his door and went off to do his huntsman duties. When the eve came round dressed in its dark blue suit, he made his way back home with the carcass of a small quail in his pack. He stumbled through the shrubbery, breaking the delicate symphony that the woods at night concoct with vegetable tunes, and once again saw his hut shimmering with light as a trail of smoke emerged from his stone chimney.

Again he made his way to the door and, finding no one around or inside his hut, he warily entered his quiet abode. As before, another warm bowl of soup sat waiting for him at the table, calling him with its aromatic tongue and appetizing scents. And, after an exhaustive search to locate the secret intruder and finding no one, tucked in mightily into his dinner and, once again, fell deep into digestive stupor.

The next morning came soaring in on the wings of a gold-tipped eagle. He decided he would make a point to get home earlier and, as the day morphed into dusk, he made his way through the thicket and the brush, this time carrying the heavy body of a young deer over his muscly shoulders.

He attempted a silent walk through the woods but his hunter boots and heavy stride gave him away over and over again. Around him, the small carcasses of twig and sprig laying in disorderly heaps across the places he passed, evidencing his evening journey and alien presence in the woody habitat.

At last he came to the clearing where his home sat and, much to his surprise, not only was his hearth ablaze and smoke rising from the chimney, he could also make out the shape of someone moving through his kitchen, coming and going in a graceful, quiet dance.

He made his way to the window and stared in astonishment.

Before his eyes, a woman of electric beauty moved in serene motion through his rugged kitchen. She touched each object with majestic reverence, as if speaking its language. As if she and matter had a secret tongue that only they could speak. He watched her chop herbs, cut carrots and stir a boiling pot over the leaping fire. And, as she tossed in the wild tarragon and the fragrant rosemary, he became captivated by the undomesticated tresses that were her hair.

A red mane sprouted from her in a fiery cascade of flaming locks that, for a moment, the hunter could not distinguish where the hearth's flames ended and where her hair began, such was the incandescence of her vermilion frizz.

He was rooted to his place and unable to move. He had been speechless until, somehow, words emerging from that fantastical place that words emerge from, words he did not know he knew, words that, even after saying them meant nothing to him, these words managed to whisper themselves into the thick tar of the evening saying, "Fox Woman dreaming."

And as the words whisked off, carried away on the backs of scurrying crickets, she turned and met his gaze steadily, warmly, mischievously telling him she knew he had been watching all along and then, welcoming him in.

He opened the door and stood at the threshold. The night around them watched in captivated excitement until, finally, they ran into each other's arms, in the embrace that only lovers know, and remained there late into the next morning.

The days unfolded in the grace that only deep love knows how to give to time. In beatific harmony, they would spend the days in ecstatic rapport and meet at night in the candor and ardor of unbridled passion.

Such was their adoration for each other that, as darkness fell, as their bodies collided in planetary merging, the stars and moon were seen peeking through their window in voyeuristic delight as they enacted the multiple ways that bodies know how to love.

The spring turned into summer with its helianthus blooms and daisy blossoms. Then the fall bounced around them in its innocent game of acrobatic leaf fall, streaking the space around them in ochre yellows and herbal reds. The winter brought to them even deeper love as their bodies searched for mutual heat in their naked embrace and then, as spring came round again, the hunter lifted his hooked nose and sniffed the air around him.

"My love," he said tenderly, "what on earth is that smell?"

She made as if she had not heard him and went on mixing flour and spices, busying herself in the labor of early morning bread making.

But his nose was not easily dissuaded and sniff he did, until he found the source of the scent perched on the wall near the entrance. The pungent smell came from a fox pelt that hung neatly on a peg of his coat rack.

"My love," he said again, his tones imitating the bread rising in the oven, so filled it was with warmth and intoxicated with yeasty love, "This thing reeks of mildew and musk. Please can we get rid of it."

The woman smiled a thin smile and buried herself into her task, not answering and letting the day unfold nonchalantly.

The hunter soon forgot about the pelt and his request. The days went on in enraptured ardor until again, his nostrils flared and the tenderness was less and he said, "My love, I asked you once. Please do as I say, get rid of that pelt, the house is bursting with its rancor."

And, for a second time, the thin smile appeared on her countenance, silent knowing filling her head and, for a second time, she did not do as she was told.

It was upon his return from a day's hunt that the odor knocked him off his feet the moment he entered his home. It pushed him about and wrestled with his large frame. The scent had taken residence in his hunter's abode. It had infiltrated the walls, had permeated the simple wooden chairs, had wiggled its wiry way into the soup bowls and the spoons. And, although he did not want to admit it, he could find the musky essence inside his nails, on the palms of his hands, in the strands of his hair.

It was then that the hunter lost all the warmth of his previously worded request. His words shot and pierced, wielding bow and arrow, brandishing blade as he exclaimed, "Woman, I will not ask you again. This is my house and you will do as I say. You will get rid of that pelt by tomorrow morning or I will get rid of it myself! Do you understand?"

To this she responded with a quiet gaze and full understanding. She nodded and agreed to do as she was told.

That night, the forest hugged itself against the well-loved walls of the hut. It stood quiet, pressing its dark eyes and leafy ears against the glassy windows, watching and listening in rapturous enjoyment as man and woman made love in fiery ecstasy and fervent passion.

As the hunter laid in post-paroxistic sleep, the woman kissed his closed eyes and whispered tender words of love and farewell. She then tiptoed to the doorway, put the pelt around her shoulders and over her head, and walked out of the hut, into the woods, into the wide mouth of night, never to be seen again.

As morning knocked on the hunter's door with its sunny knuckles, his arms reached out for the warm contours of the woman he loved. His hands met only the empty bed space, the unkind and sneering sheets, the cold room and the watermark of her absence greeting him in his dismay.

As the tumbling realization of what had occurred landed in him, he stood at the threshold, calling out into the woodlands, calling for her, aching for her to return. But the woman was far gone and would not be coming back.

All he did, from then forth, was to stand at the threshold of his forest hut, waiting.

"Now Listen. Listen to the sound of your own voice. Anchor there. Wake up. Wake up."

The End

o o o

Acknowledgements

o o o

This story came galloping onto my lap on a sunny morning in Mexico, smelling of wild mare and as alive as ripe fruit. I sat with it for a month, writing every evening as the words frolicked and danced in front of me, inviting me deeper and deeper into its living world. I came to the edge of my own learning with it, I could call it a frontier place, where I did not know where the story would go because I had not learned the lessons it contained within it in my own life.

Months went by and it lay, half-born, on my computer screen, waiting for me to catch up.

It was during my stay in Washington that I learned that sometimes stories need a midwife (or two). Mine appeared in the form of my precious friend and main editor, Johnathan Back, who graciously gifted me the boon of his intelligence, the spark of his profound inquiry, as well as the generosity of his time as we both saw the story unravel before our eyes. Johnny B, this story would not be here if it were not for you. Thank you in so many ways.

My second midwife is my darling friend, Michael Field, who first evoked my own access to primordial sound on a mountainside and then willingly listened to it roar by the side of a river, covered in moss and bark sap. If there is ever someone who has taught me the gift of friendship, presence and listening, it is you.

A Thank you of rotund depth goes to August Tarantino who pushed my capacity to receive, who answered my tentative questions and who met me at the end of the writing process with open arms and willing heart. Thank you for holding a key and being patient with me as I unlocked myself out of my own smallness. Your kindness is boundless.

Thank you, of course, to Anthony. You are my muse, you golden-robed trickster of a being.

Thank you to Mareano Ruíz whose art graces the cover of this novel. You are always a master of monstrosity, a poet of the polemic and an incredible artist to boot. I am so grateful to have gotten to collaborate on this project together.

Big dollops of gratitude to Albert Strasser for his generous help in designing the cover so artfully and lovingly, as well as for being a consistent North Star in my life.

Thank you also to Martin Shaw who first introduced the story of the "The Hunter and the Fox Woman" into my world.

A garland of appreciation to Tyler Aquarius who showed me that writing a story could be a delightful adventure. It was during the many evenings of your reading us nighttime stories that my own playful courage was born.

To my mother and father, Mike and Teté, and my brother, Pablo, for putting up with me all these years. Thank you for the steady love, the unwavering support and for the incomparable gift of calling you my family.

And lastly to the supporters and backers on the pre-sale of this book, who gave this project a generous beginning and kind support - I am indebted to you and am humbled by your kindness. May your own endeavors in life be met with endless bounty and friends like you: Barb Peterson, Kim Shirley, Patricia Saferite, Chrissie Couts, Scott Hubley, Hazel McLoughlin, Julie Taormina, Brynn Walters, Ronan McLoughlin, Japhy Dungana, Eduardo Pérez, Jeremy Couts, John Matt, Laura Dunham, Kat Lilayana Sun, Caitlin Strasser, Cian O'Reilly, Miriam Lutz, Mariel Yaghsizian, Lesly Weiner, Marisa Hope Benson, Kailey Murphy, Alan Leon, Juliana Arango, Michelle Merry, David Platoff, Danny Sherrard, Sarah Messeck, Jeremy Lynn, Hanna Tapparel, Nicole Reinhard, Jill Bailin Rembar,

Declan Ring, Carolyn Sherrard, Jordan Bartley, Jackson Isaacs, Fredrick Bøje, Mary Colleen Halley, Sue Cotter, Tarun Gudz, Claire Olivier and Alex Leverkus.

About the Author

o o o

Joy Voigt (Daniela), born in Mexico, has spent the better part of the last two decades traveling and learning across many places on the globe. Deeply passionate about the intersection between the primordial human experience and her spiritual journey, she has spent much of her life living in Buddhist Temples and meditation centers. A massage therapist by trade, she finds much of her expression through multiple mediums such as writing, making music, dancing, weaving and floral sculpture. Joy's main interest in life is learning the art of true listening.

"Fox Woman Dreaming" is Joy Voigt's fourth published book.

Please visit www.mandalasproject.com to sign up for the newsletter and to find out about upcoming releases, as well as other offerings.

Made in the USA
Middletown, DE
13 January 2022